KIN

OTHER WORKS IN DALKEY ARCHIVE PRESS'S
HEBREW LITERATURE SERIES

Dolly City
Orly Castel-Bloom

Heatwave and Crazy Birds
Gabriela Avigur-Rotem

Homesick
Eshkol Nevo

Life on Sandpaper
Yoram Kaniuk

Motti
Asaf Schurr

KIN

DROR BURSTEIN

TRANSLATED BY DALYA BILU

Series Editor: Rachel S. Harris

DALKEY ARCHIVE PRESS
CHAMPAIGN / DUBLIN / LONDON

Originally published in Hebrew as *Karov,* by Keter Books, Jerusalem, 2009

Library of Congress Cataloging-in-Publication Data

Burshtain, Deror.
  [Karov. English]
  Kin / Dror Burstein ; translated by Dalya Bilu. -- 1st ed.
     p. cm. -- (The Hebrew literature series)
  ISBN 978-1-56478-814-6 (pbk. : acid-free paper) -- ISBN 978-1-56478-793-4
(cloth : acid-free paper)
  1. Families--Israel--Fiction. 2. Adoptive parents--Fiction. 3. Birthparents--
Fiction. 4. Adult children of aging parents--Fiction. 5. Israel--Social life and
customs--Fiction. I. Bilu, Dalya. II. Title.
  PJ5055.17.U7K3713 2012
  892.4'37--dc23
                         2012033673

Partially funded by a grant from the Illinois Arts Council, a state agency

The Hebrew Literature Series is published in collaboration with The Institute for
the Translation of Hebrew Literature and sponsored by the Office of Cultural
Affairs, Consulate General of Israel in New York.

www.dalkeyarchive.com

Drawing on page 7: Uzi Katsav, charcoal on paper
Cover: design and composition by Nick Motte

KIN

I

LEAH

Once there was a big white house, and we went to the white house, and in the house there were lots of little children, teeny little children, and it was a big house, and we went inside the big house, and there were lots of children there, and one of the children had a nose like a potato, full of lumps, like some kind of old uncle, an **uncle**, not a child at all, an uncle; and there was a child with green snot smeared over her face, and a child who screamed and cried, and a child with lips the color of bitter chocolate, bitter chocolate gone bad, **yuck**, and a child with an ugly sore, and there were other children too. And I don't remember the other children, and your father definitely doesn't remember them, and I can hardly remember the child with the potato nose and the child with eyes like glass marbles, and the child who barked like a dog, and the child who crept into the stove to hide, and the uncle, we forgot the uncle a long time ago, the uncle is already dead, because there's only one child I remember, and this child was quiet as can be, and he had a little nose, and he breathed quietly, he didn't grunt or whistle, and we said at once: **this is the child**, and we pointed to this child straightaway, and we didn't take our eyes off him until they came and took him out of his cot and gave him to us and put him in our arms. And we took him in our arms and we didn't take anyone else, and we knew right away that it was you.

[   ] AND [   ]

They were sixteen. Both of them. And their parents, all four of them, like a clenched fist with only a stump left of its thumb, aged overnight. One said, "No, no." One said, "What's **this**? What's **this**?" The third said, "Out of the question. Not as long as I have any say in the matter." And the fourth spat on the floor and then bit his finger. They didn't want to hear anything. Or see anything either. So the two of them ran away to Jaffa a few weeks before the date. The journey north on the bus in her ninth month, alone, she would never forget. How she threw up next to the Ramon Crater out in the desert and all the passengers in the bus stared at her. How the driver got out and stood behind her with a glass bottle of water in his hand and asked, "Should I pour a little water on your head?" and turned to look back at his passengers with a long look. Now he really saw them. Window after window he surveyed them. Window after window. Window after window they looked back at him. Closed faces. Squashed against the windowpanes. Glinting glass. All the seats were taken except for one.

They looked again at the crumpled note, from which the sound of waves rose as from a shell. Tomorrow they were going to meet the father.

THE CITY

In two hundred and fifty million years' time the continents will be all rolled up and compressed into one mass with a kind of big salty lake in the middle, a big drop left over from the oceans of yore. And it will be very hot with hot winds blowing, and in the streets of the city that the ice will have already wiped off the face of the earth millions of years ago there will be only red sand, blazing heat, desert. And there won't be a single creature, not even spiders or germs, left in the city, the city will be empty. And all the street signs will be lying in the streets, and all the lamps will be extinguished, far below, upside down, under a layer of rocks and soil and ice and who knows what else for kilometers. Names ground into dust. Pages in the sand. A heavy red silence on the face of the earth. A few minutes pass. A decade passes. Twenty years pass. And nothing moves. Everything has stopped. Come back after a hundred years and nothing's changed. And already you almost despair. But, like a shattered vase, with a little work, the work of millions of years that is, perhaps they'll slowly be stuck together again, the pieces, like a giant jigsaw puzzle, and after maybe thirty, sixty, ninety million years, look, a squat tree, or a pale green bush, or a tiny creature swimming in some warm water. Bubbles, bubbles in the slime. Such great labor, a tree has already started to grow in a forsaken corner of the single continent, and again an asteroid strikes and annihilates the miniscule fish and the tree, or ice covers the sea again and all the creatures die, and again a time of quiescence, thirty years, thirty million, there's no clock to count it. And again a tiny fish, this time a little bigger, and with fins. And again moss on a rock. And again sweet water flows in the streams and pours into the sea. And who is this, walking there in the distance, look, it's a child, he has already entered the picture, sitting on the riverbank and doing a sum. $1 + 1 =$

Enough. Get up, Yoel. Get up. The parents are waiting.

[   ]

At the central bus station, [   ] would wait next to the buses. Sometimes for hours. Everyone passes here, he thought, so he will pass here too. "He." Nobody looked back at him.

If he could see him, only for a minute, and even from a distance, it would give him a little peace. And so in the beginning he would go and look for him. Just stand there at school fences. Is that him? Is that him? For years.

And he would sit and play at the bus station, and sometimes in the streets next to it, and sometimes people wanted to throw him a coin, but he never put out a box, and his case was closed, so nobody threw a coin, or else they put it down on the ground. One day, [   ] thought with the sound of the music in his ears, he would bend down to me with a shekel in his fingers. Everybody passes here. Yes. One day he would turn up too. He had to. The name they gave him was Emile. In 1970. But who knows what his name is now.

YOEL

Get up, Yoel, get up. And running.

Almost running, he's got a cut from shaving, he crosses the street, leaving the shade of the trees in the avenue, opposite the birdsong, the chiming of the wind chimes on the open porches, making a beeline for the fixed route share-taxi, the kids push ahead of him in the queue, he doesn't say anything, he'll wait for an empty van. One is sure to come. No, not empty, but with room for just one more. An old man gets out, Yoel gets in. Like someone penetrating a dank jungle, forging on with head lowered through the sounds echoing in the interior, yes, route 5, he sits down in the old man's place as the taxi takes off with screeching tires, orangutans shriek from the branches, a tiger slinks through dense foliage, roars, an iceberg creeps slowly from the north, a sun sits on the snowy horizon. He sits down and passes a gleaming coin to the passenger in front of him, who bends his hand backward, here, give it here.

So you tell me, Professor, the driver said to him as if continuing a lengthy conversation, is it permitted or forbidden for the driver and the passengers to have a conversation? And one of them, a pregnant woman with a bag on her knees from one of the bridal boutiques in Dizengoff Street, jumps in: In the buses they used to have stickers, it used to say, "Passengers may not stand next to the driver or talk to him while the vehicle is in motion," but I don't see any sticker there behind you, and the driver said, never mind the sticker, forget about the sticker, I'm talking to you about a principle here, is it **permitted** to talk to the driver or **forbidden** to talk to the driver? If I have an accident, said the driver, yes? if I have an accident, and we're all God forbid killed here to death, will they come and say afterwards it's because he didn't have a sticker with "It's forbidden to talk to the driver" on it? I don't understand you, Sharon, I really don't! Let me concentrate on driving, let me concentrate on the road! Let me go with the traffic flow, I'm taking a turn here now! And the woman said, pardon me, if it doesn't say that it's forbidden to talk to the driver I'll talk to the driver, and if you don't like it you don't have to answer. I take taxis specifically to talk to the driver, if I didn't want to talk to the driver I'd get onto a long bus and sit on a back seat, and the driver laughed and suddenly braked to let a cat blind in one eye cross the street.

One of the passengers, sitting behind Yoel, who had a blue inflatable felt cushion tucked under his backside and whose whole appearance shouted "senior bureaucrat" said, in your case there should be a sticker saying the opposite, "It's forbidden for the driver to talk to the passengers," and the driver said, and maybe there should be a sticker that says, "It's forbidden for the driver to read stickers"? All the passengers laughed, and Yoel laughed too, and said to the driver, can I talk to you for a minute? And the driver said, feel free, there's freedom of speech here, and the pregnant passenger said, so why have you been drumming it into my head for an hour that talking to the driver is forbidden, now you're telling him that it's permitted to talk to the driver, and she smiled at Yoel, and the driver said, sure it's permitted to talk to the driver, it depends which driver, I meant another driver. The bureaucrat shifted his position on his blue cushion and said, I've never in my life talked to the driver or stood next to the driver, I always bring a cushion and sit at the back, and Yoel turned round and asked, the cushion, is it for piles? And the bureaucrat said, not at all, the cushion is for added height, and Yoel saw that the top of his head was already pressed right up against the roof of the taxi. Hilik, you need a cushion for your head as well, how many times have I told you? Padding top and bottom, why discriminate, the driver roared with laughter as he let off an old woman, interrupting her "thank you" with a "good day," his eyes on the green light. "Hurry up, get in, there's a Jumbo behind us," he said to a couple of young women laden with packages, "but please don't talk to the driver or stand next to him!" And one of the new passengers sat down and said to her friend, Oho, my father was a bus driver for thirty years, I know those stickers by heart, "Don't put your hand or head out of the window," "Don't crack sunflower seeds—don't spit—don't litter," apparently people used to like to spit a lot, "Don't put your feet on the seats," "Passenger! Have you forgotten something on the bus?" I would copy those stickers whenever I had to write one of those "My Family" compositions at school, I would always end up writing about the bus, that's what everybody was interested in, not my mother who was a seamstress and who didn't have any stickers or anything else, only the tak-tak-tak-tak of the sewing machine, tak-tak-tak-tak from seven o'clock in the morning in the textile district, if there's a word I really hate it's "textile," but that didn't interest the teacher, the teacher always told me, give me stories about the bus, "all the children want to hear them," and once I made up a story about how they broke the windshield with the red hammer, it was utter chaos in the class, I couldn't even tell you. Yoel looked at his shoes but he was listening closely. In twenty minutes he would arrive and leave the taxi and go up to their apartment and stand before Emile's parents. And he already knew that he would stand before them tongue tied. In other words, that once more he wouldn't go up at all, that he would chicken out, like yesterday and the day before. You'll chicken out again, Zisu, he said to himself. Chicken. His tongue passed over his front teeth. I would stand behind him, every day I would come back from school with him on bus no. 5, there were no shared taxis then, and even if there were I wouldn't have taken one, because I had a free bus pass as a member of a Dan Bus Company family—and her friend interrupted her and said, which is funny, since your last name really is "Dan"—and the first one went on talking and said Shosh, don't pour salt on the wounds Shosh, my father changed our name in order to prove his loyalty to the company, a lot of drivers did that then, today nobody changes their name, but then? They changed their surnames to "Dan" and sometimes their first names too, and some of the people who rose to the highest positions in the Dan Company called themselves

"Daniel Dan" or "Dan Daniel." Right, the director of Dan was Dan Daniel and the head of the conductors' department was Danny Ben-Daniel, cried the driver, holding up the mike of his two-way radio. And my father, continued the passenger, who was only a simple driver on bus no. 5, called himself "Yaakov Dan," though everybody else called him "Kuba Dan" when they weren't just calling him plain "Dan." And he was proud of it at first, that he had the strength of character to make the change, and I would stand behind him, all my childhood I remember being in the bus behind the plastic barrier, and I would whisper to him softly, "Daddy . . . daddy . . . " but he didn't hear me, or else he just didn't answer me because talking to the driver was forbidden. He was afraid there might be an undercover inspector on the old people's seat at the front of the bus, maybe disguised as an old lady, and the minute he opened his mouth and said something to me the old lady would jump on him and give him a fine. But he would wink at me in the big scratched mirror.

And there was silence in the taxi sailing onto Rothschild Boulevard, and a soldier got off at the Dizengoff Center, and the driver rattled his collection of five-shekel coins. And the driver said, "What a life," and fell silent, and remembered the half-blind cat crossing the street and its closed eye, and he thought of Moshe Dayan, who he had once seen, when he was a young soldier, and he wanted to shout at him, Dayan, Dayan, what did you do. He pulled to a stop with the ruins of the Habima Theatre behind him. In the end I would pull the cord and the "stop requested" sign would light up and I would get off at home. He wouldn't say good-bye to me, he was too afraid of the undercover inspectors who got on the buses disguised as blind men in order to catch the drivers out, they just waited for the driver to make one little mistake and immediately got up and took him off the bus or put a reprimand in his file. And once he spat out of the driver's window, the case they made against him, Dreyfus, the disgrace . . . And what now? the friend whose name was Shosh interrupted her, and the daughter of the Dan driver said, "Now? Now he's dead."

The taxi arrived at the corner of Balfour, and Shosh said good-bye to her friend and got off, carrying a big X-ray photo in a big envelope, and the friend turned to Yoel, who didn't look at her, and said, "She's very sick. Not yet forty," and fell silent. Yoel wanted to ask her how the story about her father ended, if there was any more to it, but the woman turned away to look out of the window. Yoel turned to look at the pregnant woman in the seat behind the driver, who all this time had gone on talking to the driver and arguing with him about whether talking to the driver while he was driving was permitted or forbidden. Neither of them tired of this conversation, which seemed to have begun very long ago and might go on forever. He fixed his eyes on the woman's swollen belly. The taxi stopped in a traffic jam on the corner of Sheinkin Street. The bureaucrat's cell phone rang and he got out to answer it, apologizing for the disturbance. A colorful procession crossed Rothschild Boulevard from east to west. Yoel closed the window near him against the whistles and the drums. "Close your window," he wanted to say to the pregnant woman, "so the baby won't be startled by the noise," but he was too shy to start a conversation. The taxi was buzzing with talk. Yoel took out his MP3 player, which was a little dirty with sea sand and now contained only a few Bach organ pieces and Schubert Lieder, aside from the camera function that took up most of the memory card, and plugged in the earphones. He closed his eyes and leaned his head on the windowpane. He managed to hear the driver say, "I'm switching off the engine until they go past. It's the exodus from Egypt, except on Purim." But there was still time. A burglar alarm ripped through the air but could not penetrate the skin of his dream. People shouted outside, he didn't hear. He was tired, it was the middle of the day. Well, to be precise, he did hear the sound, to be precise, sure. He wanted to sleep, even though it was only noon. He dreamed that he was riding in a taxi and dreaming that he wanted to sleep, and what Amikam, his old father, said to him when he was small, Yoel too said in his sleep: How good it is to sleep when you're tired. A little bird flew through the taxi, entering through an open window, leaving through an open window. And other dream fragments came up and thrust themselves upon him but as usual he forgot almost everything. If he had remembered his dream he would have seen a transparent train ascending to the top of a tower, drawn by a whistling, straining iron locomotive, but when you looked at its wheels, you saw that there was nothing there, that it wasn't transparent but absent. And he woke up in an empty taxi.

Someone had forgotten a cell phone on one of the seats. The phone drilled into the cushion and its light blinked.

The taxi stood in the parking space of the new central bus station. At first the driver was nowhere to be seen, and then Yoel caught sight of him through his dazzled, freshly awakened eyes, sitting outside on a bench next to a few other drivers and drinking a hot drink from a plastic cup. Yoel's neck hurt. Vapors rose and misted the faces of the drivers and their heavy-framed spectacles. Yoel's sleep had crushed him, his neck was stiff, his MP3 player was silent and its earphones were plugged into his ears like white corks. Did you hear anything at all? Dream fragments flitted past his eyes. A window. A cloud. A whistle. A watch. He looked, without raising his leaning head, at the silent, empty taxi, at the seats on which thousands of passengers had imprinted their shapes and smells. And how sunk into themselves these seats were, he now saw for the first time, how much weight had compressed them. Compressed and deepened. He rubbed the upholstery. Like a herd of donkeys whose backs were worn and hollowed, he thought. And the taxi, like a beast of burden, drove north-south and didn't complain. Again you fell asleep, again you arrived at the central bus station, again you have to begin to go back.

Yoel got up with difficulty and climbed out of the taxi. Then he heard the driver calling him, from a distance. "Did you have a good sleep? I didn't want to wake you. You slept like a baby." And he turned to his taxi-driver friends and said to them, lowering his voice, explaining, "He fell asleep . . . " And then, after Yoel walked away and could no longer hear him, the driver added, "Him, he likes to sleep in taxis." And after a few seconds he commented gruffly to the tips of his shoes: "Him, not a week goes by that he doesn't fall asleep in my taxi." The other drivers looked at Yoel stretching himself opposite the central bus station as though it were a real spectacle.

To begin to go back again. No, he didn't have the courage to go up. But the next day he would go there again.

But the next day he would be there again, in the taxi. And he would travel all the way, alone in the taxi, thinking, why not go up today. For five shekels I could get a private taxi. But in the middle of Levinsky Street he would say to the driver, "I'm getting out here. Have a good week," and the driver, who would perhaps be the same one as yesterday, or perhaps not, would say to him, "What do you care, ride a little further, it's the same money, get off at the last stop like a human being. Who gets off in the middle of the road?" And Yoel would admit, "There's something in what you say," even though he already had one foot outside the taxi. And the trees all along Levinsky would be low and leafy and their fruit thick-skinned, and a great shadow would pass along them and through them and over the bridge, all the way to Sheinkin until it disappeared. "Are you headed back north?" Yoel would ask, and the driver would say, "Where north, I do the route, drive round in circles," and Yoel would say, "In that case, I'll go back with you."

THE CITY

After many years to come, and even more hours and minutes, the city will be a smooth surface of ice. On top of the bowling alleys, on top of the basketball stadium and all its victories and defeats, on top of the highest mall in the Middle East, on top of the sea. The ice will cover everything. And nobody skates on it, and nobody throws a snowball at the snowmen. And nobody crosses the Bosporus on foot anymore, and nobody falls asleep wrapped in thick furs anymore in a sleigh on the way from Sicily to Italy. There's nothing except for the wind and the silence. A bird frozen in mid-flight that crashed onto the plain and shattered. And wind and silence and frost. And schools of fish frozen underfoot, feet that aren't there, that don't walk anymore. That are frozen down below. Sitting on chairs. Frozen, stopped. And they don't swim, don't spawn, in the cold.

[   ] and [   ]

And once they celebrated his birthday. No, it was more than once. When he turned five and when he turned ten. When he turned five, [   ] baked him a cake, they lit candles. There was an empty chair. They sat and chewed the cake. There was a kind of damp in the house.

And when he turned ten there was a cake again. The same chair. The same cake, to tell the truth. She kept the recipe. But they brought out a kind of doll and put it on the chair. The hot candles dripped onto the chocolate icing. They threw the whole cake into the garbage. With the candles and all those disgusting candies.

The next day the doll disappeared.

YOEL

And over the years the lack of resemblance between Emile and his parents became more pronounced. If when he was a baby it was still possible to pretend that his skin color was still changing, that it was a temporary infantile darkness that would pass, at the age of three Emile walked between them and everyone who saw them noticed the contradiction. And the children pointed, and parents bent down to explain. No, don't point . . .

There was an internal contradiction in their home. A guest had entered the family on a permanent basis.

And one day Yoel went to the barber and dyed his hair coal black. But the fairness of his stubble exposed the deception on the very same day, and he started shaving twice a day to stop it from growing.

Leah was silent, she stood in the doorway of the barbershop, half of her outside. She averted her face from the strong smell.

The next day he got up again and went down to the avenue and crossed Yehuda HaMaccabi Street, and got into a no. 5 share-taxi again. He rubbed the five-shekel coin. A tin coin, he thought, definitely, a tin coin, and he paid the driver with the five shekels, and although he was entitled to a reduction of one shekel as a senior citizen he didn't ask for it, and for a moment he was gratified by the fact that the driver, this time too, didn't offer him a reduction and didn't give him a shekel back, as most of the drivers did (in fact the reduction had been canceled in January, but he didn't know this, and it would be some time before he asked, aren't you going to give me a reduction for seniors, and the driver would look at him, by then it would be August already, and say, are you joking? It was canceled in January, now there aren't any seniors/ non-seniors anymore, now everyone's a senior). He sat on his seat, his face turned to the window, when the taxi recklessly passed a bus and got on Dizengoff. He could easily have closed his eyes and seen, sometimes even without closing them, the orange grove that once stood in the place where a number of bridal shops were now crowded, but he wasn't interested. How he hated the sinking into memories common to all his friends in his age group, they sank further and further into the past, always and immediately dragging him into conversations about what had already happened, looking at the streets and teasing out images from the past, before the city existed, when everything was still open and "ours," living in their memories as much as possible, thought Yoel nodding glassy-eyed at a funny story. And every word led to bygone days, mostly to wars, to the establishment of the state, he was eleven then, remember how we were children when Ben Gurion spoke, you remember the declaration of independence, do I remember, I was there, I stood on an orange crate, they would sink into reminiscence and reminiscence would give way to invention, and Yoel would keep quiet and wait for them to disperse, until he stopped going to meet the "old crowd," he couldn't stand it, how after a few greetings and perfunctory questions someone would throw some ancient code word onto the table, next to the sunflower seeds, for instance the name of a commanding officer in the Six-Day War (Yoel, of course, had dodged the draft, run away to Holland, and they knew it, which was why they kept coming back to it, he thought, asking him innocently, "So you parachuted to the Western Wall did you?" and laughing themselves sick inside), and so immediately dive backward in time, looking away and sinking into the "good old days," you remember the waitress at the Hungarian blintzes place, do I remember, what was her name, Paula, Polina? didn't we eat there after Yoshua married Tzipa? Yoshua from the overseas mobilization, what are you talking about, Yoshua left the country right after the Yom Kippur War, he left the country but he left his arm behind him in the sands of Sinai, no, I'm talking about the Yoshua from Kfar Yoshua, so, what about him, he married Tzipa Wilensky at the blintzes place, that's what about him, so, what's the connection? We were talking about the blintzes, that's the connection, but I'm talking about Yoshua Ben Meir, Haika's platoon commander from the overseas mobilization, ah, that's another Tzipa completely, you're mixing them up, I'm talking about "Tzipa harmonica," what are you talking about, she married that millionaire, the Persian, what's his name, the arms dealer, who was in the "Mahanot Olim" youth movement . . . Yoel, you kept in touch with Yoshua's Tzipa, didn't you? After he left the country? After he bought the coal cargo?

And Yoel said: No. No, I don't remember anything.

The taxi crawled along Dizengoff. Or perhaps the taxi stopped and the street crawled backward.
Suddenly, the thought of heavy snow. Heavy snow, heavy snow. He closed the window.

Brides-to-be stood in front of big mirrors and examined their breasts and the way they fitted into the cut of their dress. Grooms stood aside and measured them with eyes in which a hint of disappointment could already be read. They look at themselves the way their men would look at them, he thought, and he looked at the enormous breasts of one of the brides, which appeared duplicated in the mirror like the stuffing for a leather sofa, until the taxi took off and drove away while the bride searched the street with her eyes and met the gaze of another man replacing that of Yoel, who looked at her and licked his lower lip, and she stuck out her tongue at him. On the second floor of one of the bridal shops he saw a sign: "The aesthetic bride—enlargements!!—liposuction—lips now at bargain prices," and from the entrance to the building a mother and daughter emerged, both with their faces bandaged, supporting each other, looking frightened. He tried to recall Leah's bridal gown but he couldn't remember anything except that it was white. And he wasn't really sure of this either. The rabbi held a glass of wine to his lips. The taxi passed the clinic where Leah had gone for tests. Now there was a florist there. And when she emerged from the clinic with a look that was ashamed but aimed apologetically at him, he understood that the problem wasn't with her. Bunches of flowers burst forth from the shop. And suddenly he remembered stories from the Bible. All the barren women. And the prayers. And God heard them and made them fruitful. Leah came up to him and took both his hands. Suddenly her dress took on different colors in his eyes. Now it turned black. All his adult life Yoel had feared sterility, and now, at the age of seventy, he couldn't avoid the thought that his obsessive thoughts about sterility, which had started at the age of fifteen or a little earlier and accumulated in his head and body during all those years, had turned in the end into a self-fulfilling prophecy. From the thought to the brain and from the brain to the body, in other words to the reproductive system, to the sexual organ. Because it accumulates. Whenever they had sex, Yoel looked at the bride who bent down to pick up a long glove, and for some reason it didn't go well, he would think to himself, now I'm going to get my punishment, I failed, it will show in the results. He didn't really believe this, which is to say he was afraid of it, which is to say he didn't know, after years of brooding about it, what the truth was. But he always took care to laugh to himself at his thoughts. The main thing is not to take it seriously, said Yoel, and everything will be all right. But it wasn't all right. The mother and daughter got into the taxi and squeezed into the back seat. Both of them, Yoel noticed, had enormous, erect breasts under their T-shirts, and big, prominent nipples, really swollen, and the size of their breasts, he noticed with his engineer's eye, was without a doubt absolutely

31

identical, although in the case of the daughter, who was very thin, they looked larger. An optical illusion, he thought. The mother tapped him on the shoulder and he turned round. She pushed ten one shekel coins into his hand and said, "Can you pass this to him? Two. And a receipt for the ten." He measured her body with an ostensibly indifferent eye, ignoring her face and the big bandage covering the bridge of her nose, which was just like her daughter's. At least she was hers, no doubt about it. That is, the daughter. She was hers and they would grow more and more alike. The daughter would become more womanly, the mother would grow younger and younger. They would have the same nose, the same breasts, they would go to the gym together and their bodies would be the same body. And he thought: maybe we should do the same thing too. I'll get a tan on a tanning bed, we'll go down to the Golden Ratio plastic surgery clinic—get your eyelids done—leg shortening without anesthetic—ingrown toenails—and it will hurt, and they'll cut us up, and there'll be disinfectant, harsh but necessary, but they'll cut according to plan, and when we come out and get into a share-taxi and I pay with two five-shekel coins we'll be a proper father and son at last. And people will see it, too. You'll see it, he wanted to say, but to whom.

Far behind, in Dizengoff, a little bit of cold breathed out of the open shops. The street itself stank like a dump.

The mother and daughter were swallowed up under the trees in Balfour Street, and Yoel thought that he had better get off before the avenue came to an end and the taxi reached the area of the central bus station. On no account did he want to end up there. In other words, that was where he was supposed to end up. And he said, "Nachmani Street please," and the driver pretended not to hear because he wanted to catch the green light and he said, "What?" and Yoel said, "I want Nachmani, please," and the driver said, "What, here?" and stole another few meters, for no reason, and then stopped after turning into Bezalel Yaffe Street. Which was where he liked to stop.

It was very quiet in Tel Aviv on that day. There was no explanation for this.

Yoel stood up to get out and suddenly, for no particular reason, he turned to the driver and said, "I want to say something to you, sir," and the driver looked at the green light and said in a Bukharan accent, and with obvious impatience, "Well, what," and Yoel said, "I wanted to thank you for the ride, I had a very comfortable ride. Anyone can see that you're a professional driver." And the driver looked at him for a moment, trying to decide if the white-haired passenger was setting a trap for him, and his right hand gripped the handle attached to the nickel rod that opened and closed the door. And his short thick fingers opened and closed on the worn nickel handle, and he said to Yoel, after some hesitation and a long look, "You know what?" and there was a long pause, and he stared though the front window at the traffic light, which turned orange and suddenly red, "Seven years I'm driving this taxi, **seven years**, and nobody ever said anything like that to me before. Not ever." And he went on staring at Yehuda Halevi Street for a few seconds, and Yoel raised his hand in embarrassment. And when he raised his hand the taxi began to drive very slowly, as if reluctantly, and Yoel sensed the driver's eyes fixed on his back. And he thought, if I lower my hand he'll stop and reverse towards me. For sure. And he lowered his hand.

[   ]

Ten years after she gave him away the idea of having another child came up. They were twenty-six, both of them. "The difficult period" was already ostensibly behind them. They wanted to turn a new page. There was a smell of cigarettes in the house, the walls breathed in the smoke day and night. Breathed it out. They decided to quit. They quit. For a month or two. They painted the walls white. And she tried to get pregnant. But the walls coughed. The walls were giving up smoking. Black walls. Suffocating walls. Black lung-walls. Coal. They had various copper vessels full to the brim. Ashtrays. The house wouldn't let her.

Every day she went downstairs and tipped all the stubs into the garbage. Knocked the copper against the bin. But when she went up again the stench would hit her in the stairwell.

YOEL

No, he wanted to go on working, without a break, even on the long nights, that's what he said to the company director, how did the word "long" get out, damn, a mistake, a mistake . . . but in his heart he tried to be glad about being forced out, and he saw himself, his wallet bursting with pension money and severance pay exchanged for foreign currency, traveling the world with a light bag and a light coat and a pocket camera, looking at airplane and train schedules, not in a hurry, falling asleep on a train on a cold night in Budapest and waking up the next morning in Venice opposite boats and big lit canals and the water of the Great Canal rippling in front of his opening eyes. Two months after his retirement Yoel was still trying to realize this freedom, for the first time after decades of work under elevated roads, a yellow helmet on his head, shouting at foremen, holding blueprints, always mistakes the minute he turned his back. In his dream he drives on his own over highway interchanges he was responsible for building, like the Netanya interchange, driving alone in his new jeep, in daylight, knowing that the bridge is about to collapse, sticking his arm out of the top of the vehicle in order to hold onto something when he falls, a tree branch or laundry line, and he knows that there's nothing there but nevertheless he stretches his arm through the open roof, even though he knows, in his dream, that the jeep isn't a convertible, but the roof opens and he feels the strong wind on his hand, and he goes on driving a little longer and he counts, one, two, three, and goes on counting more and more until he hears the bridge crumbling under his wheels, and for a second he sees the blueprint in his mind's eye and identifies the fault, and it was his mistake, and he knows it. His mistake. And then the car begins to lose height and tip forward toward certain destruction, he's already stopped counting but he hears his voice going on as if on a soundtrack, and he stretches his arm a little further and utters a long kind of aaahhhh until someone takes his hand and pulls him out of the car. Now too, in the spring of 2007, after his retirement, a few days before his seventieth birthday, the dream sometimes came back, and he would wake up in the morning and look at the apartment, which now seemed emptier, and he would go outside to the avenue and get onto a no. 5 share-taxi and ride to the south of the city, sometimes even at five in the morning, while Emile was still sleeping, and he'd get off mostly between Nachmani and Balfour Streets and walk around there, showing his pensioner's card to an invisible audience, walking slowly down the avenue or in the streets and looking at the trees and the shop windows, wandering aimlessly and thinking to himself never mind, some great idea would grow out of this idleness, perhaps a story, and he would write it all down at once, in a café, and publish it. When he was a child Yoel could draw the coastline of the Mediterranean Sea with astonishing accuracy. And now, in the café, he tried to draw it again. His pen rose north from the Haifa Bay and already he's in Greece, and already he stops to put in Cyprus, goes back up, to Italy, adds the islands. And the more sea and harbors appear, the younger he grows. And joyfully he reaches the Straits of Gibraltar, and skips a little lower down, how he had imagined swimming across these straits as a child, with his parents standing on either side leaning down and applauding him, shouting, over the sea, as indeed they did, but it was over his desk. And he begins his return journey, stopping at Djerba, Tripoli, Alexandria, the smell of fish, and suddenly a great desire to sit opposite the sea and eat olives and honey.

He stood up and sat down again. He went to the ATM. Withdrew a large sum. And put it in an envelope. He would count it at home. The exact amount.

And he wrote down, in another notebook, lists of things he noticed, for example, the tendency of young girls to wear very low-slung pants and tattoo something in a triangular pattern on their lower backs, a tattoo that called for a whole new wardrobe, low trousers and high tops, which of course called for a radical diet and the tanning of ordinarily hidden areas, and mainly, thought Yoel, a boundless readiness for sexual adventurism. He made notes on the subject of cellular telephones, and remembered how when he was a child there was a man who talked to himself out loud on the street until one day an ambulance stopped next to him and took him away, whereas now it was the people who didn't talk to themselves who were the minority. Going past on the avenue were more and more young, energetic men and women, all of them suddenly thin, Yoel noticed and wrote down, tall and muscular and shaven headed. All the men shaven headed in skinny pants, all the women with big breasts, he noticed, and a tattoo on their lower backs or on their shoulders. All of them suddenly making money, all suddenly healthy and young, all in fast new cars, all sitting in cafés. Above all he was astonished by the number of people in cafés in the middle of the day, young people who would once have been at work and now they were drinking coffee and talking on cell phones and not sweating even in the middle of August. They never left the air-conditioning. Big breasts and a little blue light in their ears where once they would have stuck a flower. And he didn't understand what they were saying. As if Hebrew had been changed into some other language. He was sure that it was Hebrew, but he didn't understand much of anything that the young people said, they spoke so fast, and the accents sounded foreign. Attached to their ears they had instruments flickering with blue light and they talked loudly and walked with brisk steps, waving one hand in the air, and to Yoel it seemed a spectacle of utter madness, apocalyptic, even though he knew very well that there was nothing more natural, that a person from the eighteenth century would look at him in exactly the same way, if Yoel were standing under an overpass or talking on the phone at home. A wind swept dry leaves onto the asphalt path between the houses. He went into a stairwell and sat down. He opened the notebook with his story, wrote the date carefully on the first page and put the notebook back in his bag.

* * *

In the first days after his retirement he would sit at home facing the avenue and stare at the treetops. Birds screeched, quarreling in the foliage. Music. It was hard to concentrate. Books. A page, two pages. And suddenly he stood up. Thinking about the city and its future. Worried by the summer in December. And once the taxi driver said, "We have to really fuck 'em, the Arabs, not only in Lebanon," and Yoel suddenly rose furiously to his feet and moved to the door and got out and was nearly run over. And he knew that he was waiting in unacknowledged suspense for a phone call from the office, and the telephone that didn't ring somehow seemed to ring anyway, there was a silent ringing in the house. And he turned away from the tree and looked at length at the old black telephone, a heavy rotary-dial phone that he insisted on using even though it made so much noise and in spite of the new telephones with their buttons and short cuts and then those cell phones with all their memories and cameras. The telephone was silent and Yoel got up and went to check if it was connected to the wall, but he checked nonchalantly, as though absentmindedly, as if to show that it didn't really bother him. He pushed the plug, but the plug was firmly in place. During his last weeks at work, when his young replacement had already started running around both the office and the building sites with his two telephones and his palm computer, Yoel had imagined his retirement as a great convalescence, but in its first days he actually felt like someone who had just fallen ill, not a severe illness but a bout of flu, throat a little sore, lower-back pains too, no need to stay in bed, no high fever, but something not right nevertheless, something out of joint, a slight pressure in his head. As if after swimming in the Amazon all your life, one morning you found yourself in the Yarkon. Now you're in the Yarkon, he thought, and wrote in his notebook, "Go for a row on the Yarkon," "Suggest it to Emile," because you won't be able to row the boat alone. And he knew that he wouldn't suggest it, and he knew that Emile wouldn't agree. And he felt his arms and said to them, "What a pair of sticks." And he remembered how they'd sailed on the Yarkon, he and Emile and Leah, in a wooden boat, when was it, maybe the beginning of '74, after they returned from the three-month trip they'd begun the night of Yom Kippur. And Yoel rowed and Emile fell asleep at the bottom of the boat, and Yoel stopped rowing for a minute and let the boat move of its own accord, and both of them looked at him lying there in the sunlight as the air moved through his green shirt. And he heard Leah's voice saying to the water, "What a boy," and suddenly he picked up the phone.

YOEL

He didn't look like him, he was a brown baby. Yoel said to Leah: Yes, we'll take him, look at his fingers. And his eyes, look how he's examining you. And they decided on the child in less time than it would take them to decide on the Peugeot or the new apartment on the eighth floor they would buy a few years later "on paper." We made up our minds quickly, thought Yoel, because we knew that if we started to hesitate we'd be lost. Our doubts would have destroyed us and we wouldn't have been able to decide, because every minute another reason would come up for or against. And, altogether, the looks of the other children, those eyes, all of them deserved to be taken, all of them were good children, we couldn't have gone on standing there more than a few minutes, you could go crazy if you tried to take in all of them, to think of their futures. But he thought too: They must grow into monsters there. When time passes and nobody comes to take them. After a year. After five years. And some of them probably have to be strapped to their beds. And what did you expect, he said quietly to the hospital logo on the curtain, that we would adopt sixty, seventy children?

Yoel buttoned his shirt. Behind the curtain the doctor typed something with one finger on his new, cordless keyboard, the tip of his tongue sticking out, his glasses on his forehead, his eyes narrowed with effort under a plastic sculpture of a very big, open eye, and next to it a smaller relief of the digestive system. In his mind's eye Yoel saw a picture of an interchange with a tangle of streets leading right and left, tied up into itself with a butterfly bow. The stabbing came again. He let out a brief cry, Oh! The doctor didn't hear him. Yoel stepped out from behind the curtain.

"Sit down, Zisu . . . have a look at this graph, I'll turn the screen toward you . . . technology today is really something, I'm connected to the central computer on the Internet . . . all the patients are connected to me . . . today everybody's seriously ill, I'm seriously ill myself, my leg is killing me, as a doctor I'm supposed to have a different attitude, but just look at the kind of leg I was given, one healthy leg and one very sick one, they give me injections straight into the sick leg, you know, Zisu, and once they injected the healthy leg, and then the healthy one got sick too . . . who can trust doctors today . . . as a doctor I . . . what? What? Speak clearly, don't mumble."

And then Yoel saw this picture: he, Yoel, on a cold metal surface, naked and dead, eyes closed, lying there limply, but he looks at him, at himself, through a kind of round netted window, and he feels ashamed of his exposed flesh, and he sees that his genitals are visible too, shrunken and pathetic, and people walk past indifferently, the people who work in the morgue, a nurse, doctors, the security guard, the janitor, and he realizes that he doesn't feel at all sorry for this death, no sorrow at all, only shame, a kind of disgrace, why don't they cover him with a sheet.

A few days later they sat on the balcony of the apartment that overlooked the synagogue in Smuts Avenue. The child lay in a cradle. "We did well," said Yoel, and Leah said, "He chose us." The sterile Yoel Zisu. And suddenly he stood up, went to the front door with a marker in his hand, and added Emile's name to the little sign. And then he wrote over their two names as well. And hastily, like a thief, he drew a cloud to frame the three names.

A solitary old neighbor peered at him small-faced through the peephole on the far side of the hall.

He remembered now, sitting on a bench in Rothschild Boulevard, how he imagined then, on the balcony, his sperm pouring out of his penis and seeping into the baby's body, and soaking into it, or how during the night he would pick the baby up and set him carefully between his wife's legs, and the baby would slide in easily, and he would wait for him there until daybreak, until he came out and was born.

Passersby cast doubt on the child.

And so he would draw him into a secluded garden, so they wouldn't keep looking all the time. And they would be hidden among the trees. It was a botanical garden in the north of the city. And he thought of it as a secret garden. And once they saw a blind man in the garden, groping his way along the paths with his white stick. And Yoel wanted to go up, to help, and in the end he called out to him, "Hey, Mister, do you need any help there," and the blind man answered him, "Stay with the child, Baba, there's no problem, I just have to take a piss, don't look." And he stood next to a big oak. Yoel averted his eyes. But he heard the sound of the piss on the fallen leaves.

And he thought suddenly of the sea, how he once sat facing the Pacific Ocean, when he was an engineering student in California. Fields of flowers. And he looked round and there was nobody there, and at first he felt afraid, and afterward he spread out his arms and shouted, full of joy, and he didn't look to see if anyone had come in the meantime, and he didn't care if anyone saw him. On the contrary, he wanted people to see. Cars streamed along the expressway on the other side of the garden's low wall. You have to look at every road as the distant continuation of some junction or other, he thought, some interchange, and then everything becomes clear, the picture becomes a big picture. At the end of this garden is our sea and at the end of the sea is an ocean, he thought. They're connected. People think of every road as if it has a beginning and an end. But no, when one road ends another one begins, and even before it begins there's another road, and thus like tributaries of rivers they stream slowly on until they reach the big junctions and overpasses and interchanges, and collect in the lakes that are the big parking lots next to the sea.

Another blind man came into the garden and started to feel the leaves. Emile looked at him and gripped the hem of Yoel's coat.

His fingers dug into it. Into the rough fabric. And the warm round button. And the frayed threads. And the holes in the button.

YOEL

Next to the beach the two of them stood, [   ] and [   ], waiting for him. A crow pecked at his heart. Because he saw Emile in their faces. Because Emile looked like both of them, him and her. Even from a distance. The way they stood, the movements of their hands, their bowed heads—were his. No, not mine. And a burning insult flooded Yoel, undermined him, slowly disintegrated him. Everything came from there. From them. They even gave him his name. He was him and her too. Yoel's eyes skipped from him to her. Yes, they were his parents, no doubt about it. What were their names? Like a door opening. Skies clearing. His eyes darted between them, he broke into a sweat, he went on walking toward them, understanding that he recognized them because of their obvious resemblance to Emile, whereas they did not recognize him. He could walk past them and they wouldn't have any idea. For a moment it seemed to him that the man not only looked like Emile but was his actual, older twin, whereas the woman didn't look like him at all, and then, a second later,

Yoel saw that there was actually an astonishing resemblance be-tween Emile and the woman. Although she was a woman, she was Emile—her eyes were his, her hair was his, though his eyes and his hair were his as well. Altogether, they looked alike, thought Yoel, they resembled each other and therefore both of them resembled Emile. And a second later, they didn't look like each other, only the man, only the woman looked like him. It didn't stop. Emile's face flickered over his parents' faces. Yoel couldn't hold on to it for even a second, put his finger on the resemblance, on the feature that belonged beyond a doubt to the child who had been with him for thirty-seven years.

The go-between had refused to tell him their names. He'd ar-ranged for them to meet on the street corner, the day and the hour, come to the corner of Yarkon and Yona Hanavi, good luck to you and my job is done. Yoel gave the go-between an envelope with a "nice sum" and said "You can count it" and lowered his eyes. But the go-between said, "No . . . we have complete confidence in you, sir," and with two fingers he opened the flap of the envelope and peeked with one eye closed, with his mouth twisted sideways.

The two of them stood there, looking emphatically at their watches, as if to signal the fact of their waiting to everybody who saw them. Yoel kept his eyes on the pavement. He wouldn't stop, he couldn't stop just like that and address these people. Suddenly the whole plan seemed insane to him. What was he doing, who do you think you are, thirty-seven years, leave it alone. Look at them, simply say-ing the word, simply bringing up the idea, that's already a crime. He fixed his eyes on the pavement and went on walking. There was a loose paving stone under his foot and for a moment he lost his balance. Walk straight past, go to the beach, come a little late. You've seen them, that's something anyway. Run away, cancel the whole thing. They won't know who you are, they'll call the go-between, they'll yell at him, he'll try to contact you, he'll forget all about it, he's already received his fee. Go on walking, breathe normally, raise your head, don't look suspicious. What a crazy idea, what were you thinking? Think that you're on a bridge and they're underneath it. Keep on walking, go past them, don't give any sign that . . . And already his lips are pursed for a nonchalant whistle. A lot of people are walking past here, why are they all in fancy dress, why has that little girl got wings, is it already Purim? Why is it so hot? And he raised his head like someone out for an innocent stroll and walked past them with a quick, light step, looking ahead at the water. They turned their heads and said in unison, half questioning, half stating a fact: Excuse me, Emile's father,

YOEL–[   ] AND [   ]

They stood next to the signpost, all three of them holding on to it
like sailors to the mast of a ship. The sea was close. And he wished
he could go down to the water, wade in deep, and let it wash over
him. The signpost showed the way. And he was afraid, that's the
truth, to look at them. As if the look itself, their faces, would con-
stitute a claim of ownership, and also the guilt, yes, also the guilt.
Even though if there was a guilty party here it was **them**, thought
Yoel. But their guilt was already subject to the statute of limita-
tions. And even though they were the ones who had abandoned
the child, and he was the one who had rescued Emile from the fate
of a government orphanage, and without hesitation pointed to the
child and said, **that one**, immediately, as if he had already decided
in advance and there was no need to look at him any longer, nevertheless he still felt guilty. Like a thief. Like—

They told him their names and their surname but he couldn't
catch the names and asked again, and in his mind they remained

as square brackets on a printed page, square and empty. Of the surname he remembered nothing but the letter S. He asked them their names again and forgot them again, and he was embarrassed to write them down. They had normal names, that he remembered, something like Avraham or Moni or Motti or Eliezer for the husband and Rachel or Malka or Esther for the wife. And as if they had come to a decision to do so, all three of them let go of the mast and began to sail toward the sea, a matter of two minutes, rowing down the river of Yona Hanavi Street.

At first he walked next to them, a little apart, and then, because of various obstacles on the pavement, a garbage bin or dog shit, they got mixed up, and sometimes he walked next to the wife (what was her name? what was her name?) and sometimes next to the husband. If anyone had looked at them he would no doubt have concluded that together they were an estate agent and his clients emerging from an apartment for rent and walking together to argue over the price. And there was a kind of dance there, a trio, a kind of street tango, from time to time one of them lightly touching another like three beads in a shoe box in the hands of a child. She couldn't help it, suddenly she thought that Yoel was actually her husband. It was as if she knew him. Juices rose to her brain, electricity fizzed and blinked there. And he, the father, looked at Yoel and thought exactly the same thing, that she, his wife, may have gone to bed with him. Cheated on him then, all those years ago, and given Emile to her lover. A conspiracy. Of course they didn't really believe it, these were thoughts running around their heads, passing from head to head. And there was also, for a brief moment, a kind of scene in which all three of them suddenly saw him, their Emile, walking next to them. But Yoel saw him closer to the way he really looked, approaching the age of forty. And they, who didn't know what he looked like, imagined him as a baby floating above the pavement, like the birds that sometimes accompany us on our way to the sea.

Show us a picture of him? asked the mother after a long hesitation. Yoel went through his wallet, took out an old photograph, he was eight years old in it. The husband took out a handkerchief and mopped up some spilled coffee. "Take it, you take it." He couldn't look at it. And then Yoel remembered, slapped his forehead, and took out his iPod, opened the folder "Emile" and showed them the presentation he had prepared, four pictures a year, including scanned pictures from the age of one week, a hundred and fifty photographs. And every three seconds a new picture came up and replaced the one before.

Yoel turned to the sea. A Phoenician boat loaded with cedar beams made its way diagonally from Tyre to Carthage. Three high purple flags beat in his eyes. He wanted to vomit.

And they saw him growing slowly before their eyes on the little screen. Yoel didn't dare look at their faces gazing gravely, dry-mouthed. And so he turned to look at the sea or the sand dunes. Pulled out the white earphones nervously and put them away. Every few seconds a year passed. After a few minutes Emile was already sixteen, and the wife said, turn it back a minute, I didn't see properly, but the husband said, no, don't stop, let him run. He didn't go into the army, thought the father and looked at his wife for a second. The last pictures came up. Yoel brought his eyes back hesitantly. And they went on staring at the screen even after the presentation was over and the iPod switched itself off. He reached out for the device but they didn't notice. After a few seconds the husband said, give it to him, and the wife suddenly stood up and walked quickly into the men's bathroom, which was closer to the place where they were sitting. Yoel and the father went on sitting in silence, Yoel playing with his switched-off iPod, the father looking at the ice-cream stand. Yoel thought, who knows if she won't run away and leave us alone together. She'll escape through the bathroom window and she won't come back. The mother came out of the toilets with her hair wet. Her husband stood up when she approached the table and then sat down again. Yoel said, "This is something else, eh?" and fell silent in embarrassment. The husband said, "So . . . how, um, what can we actually do for you?" and Yoel took out his earphones and plugged them back into the iPod. "The things they've got today," said the father to the wet forehead. They both thought, maybe he can make us a copy, but then they thought, immediately, that this wasn't a good idea, it wasn't a good idea to have it in the house, because once it was in the house they wouldn't be able to go out anymore. Yoel said, "Do you want to see it again?" And they said at once, both of them together, "No, no." And Yoel tapped his foot and said, "I don't know how to say this . . . " and the mother cut him short in a hard voice, "You don't have to say anything, we understood on our own. You want us to meet him, right? So we've decided. We're not meeting the child," and the father said, as if to soften her words, "We got some advice."

And Yoel said, alarmed, "No, no, wait a minute. Just a second . . .
let's move a little closer to the sea . . . "

*   *   *

Look, listen to me, he pleaded, even though they were already
listening as hard as they could, listen to me, he said, wait a second. No, no, he said. No, that's not it, he said. No, no. Not that,
he explained. I want you to take him. He doesn't know anything,
nothing, not a thing . . . I want you to have him back. I want you
to have him, to have him back and take him home. I've already
thought through the details, tell me what you think, I thought you
should take him to my apartment. I mean, for you to have it. What
I'm saying is, I'll give him the apartment, no, no, I'll give it to you,
as a gift. I've already prepared all the papers, I thought of all the
details, all I need is your particulars. Suddenly the title deeds appeared and then he put them back in his bag. You'll live there,
he's already used to it there. I want him to live with you. You're
his parents after all, why lie to ourselves. Look, it's so logical. I'm
older than you by how many, twenty years more or less? If he stays
alone now (my wife? she passed away long ago, when he was six,
she fell . . . we had, um . . . an accident, I'll tell you about it later,
never mind now, listen to me a minute, let me explain), if he stays
alone now, he'll be an orphan. I'm sick, it's here in my stomach, I
may not live to see next spring. No, it doesn't matter, I've done my
job. What? A traffic engineer, overpasses and interchanges. But
it doesn't have to be that way, right? Because he still has parents.
You! You're his parents. Forget the past. All three of us only want

what's best for him, right? What I'm saying is this, we can give him another twenty years of having a father and a mother. I'm not talking about turning the clock back, there's nothing magical about it, I'm offering you a concrete proposal, I'm outlining a simple plan. I've put money away for him too, he won't be a burden on you. And I'll compensate you. I'll transfer the apartment on Smuts to you. Where do you live? Levinsky? I built an overpass on Levinsky . . . so you'll move to the north, is that bad? A nice avenue. Opposite the synagogue. You can live there. With him. But you don't have to, no! No! You could just keep in touch, hear how he's doing, and he'll go on living there alone, no, however things work out, however things work out, I'm not telling you what to do. All I want is that when I go I'll know that he isn't alone. That he'll have your phone number, that if he needs anything . . . I'll get you cell phones too, I'll put his photos in the phones, I thought of all the details, you can't imagine the happiness, knowing that you can take your leave and your child will have a soft landing. We have a rare opportunity here, let's say that all these years you were, how to put it, supplementary parents. Yes, yes, supplementary parents, supplementary parents. In reserve, waiting for him on the sidelines. I have such respect for you, for waiting, for waiting all these years. I'm not a sentimental man, but I want to hug you, you, I owe you so much, you saved my life, you gave me a great gift, we . . . The father patted him lightly on the shoulder. They looked at him and then at each other. Yoel recovered, put the tissues away in his bag. Now I've kept the child safe for you for thirty-seven years, and from now on you'll take him and everything will be for the best. We'll work out the legalities, that's no problem.

Because there's no other possibility, it simply doesn't make sense for a child to remain alone in the world when he has two parents, and in the same city too, so close, right? There are such dangers here . . . there's no time . . . it could happen tomorrow, he was shouting suddenly, or next month, who knows.

He dried his sweat, but new sweat broke out in its place. They too dried their sweat. The sea was so close. No wind blew. They sat next to the sea and shivered.

THE CITY

The sea will flood it, at first only the outskirts, like a girl when the skirt of her white dress gets dirty at the hem, and at first she takes the trouble to clean it, but afterward she has no option but to cut it off, and the skirt gets shorter. Salt water is already bubbling in the houses, boats fleeing east, climbing against the current. First the pillars, then the first floors, like a giant thermometer when the mercury climbs higher and higher as the delirious patient's fever rises. The birds will sense the threat and escape to the mountains. A stampede of insects against the direction of the sun. And still the level rises. Like a tap dripping in the yard. But the tap too soon covered with water. A big tap, a giant tap. A tap whose diameter measures a kilometer. And you can hear the pressure build. Drop by drop. And after many years the fish will swim through the roof-top apartments, past abandoned aquariums, coming home, as it were, to the sea that will wrap them like a gift. And there will be deposits of salt on all the roofs. And schools of blue whales in the skyscrapers and between them. On the vast surface of the sea big bubbles will rise from time to time, drowned cities barely breathing, suffocating. And big gold coins sunk deep in thick sand, under broken chests with locks of rust under great ships without prows. Far from there a key rests at the bottom of the sea, bearing all the weight of the water. And the drowned pass by without uttering a sound, slowly, silently, as if swimming in slow motion, standing up.

[   ], [   ], Yoel

They sat at an out-of-date computer, an ancient green screen, slow modem. 117 Levinsky Street, Tel Aviv. [   ] opened his mouth to say something, she shushed him, as though not to disturb the computer at its work. They fixed their eyes on the pale green screen. "Wait, let it do its work . . . " And like a very fat bird of prey, heavy and grunting, limping in the air on an invisible bridge, heavy-winged, the email struggled through, drifted in thin threads. And after a second and a half the bird landed on the windowsill and fell into Yoel's apartment.

It's from them, he knew before he opened it. He opened the message. It held only one word, which they had written in English, in case he had a problem with Hebrew: no.

[   ]

And the thing was that they didn't understand what his problem was. After all, he wasn't the one who had given birth. The few people who had asked turned to **her**, asked **her**. And after a few years nobody asked her either. They wanted to forget, they forgot. But once friends came, sat a while in the living room, cracked sunflower seeds, drank. And they asked her. The lamp was above his head. His wife gave the usual answers. She didn't want them to talk to her about it. And in fact mostly they said nothing. But this time they insisted, asked her questions. And she answered them. She told them the truth. After that they never saw them again. But then she talked. And as she talked she remembered her dream, that someone was cutting her up. Like cloth. And she told them that too. The words broke out of her. Like the sound of big, iron scissors.

And he sat and listened. And then he suddenly switched off the lamp over his head. And they didn't notice that the light had gone out over him. So he sat there, in semi-darkness, and waited.

YOEL

Every Friday Yoel would settle into the armchair in the living room, "to read," and fall asleep after a few minutes, mostly without opening his book. He would hold the book, usually a thick volume that he hadn't succeeded in plowing through for years now, books whose first five pages he had read maybe twenty times, and still hadn't grasped what they were supposed to be about. And once he asked Emile, tell me, all this literature, what's it good for? And Emile looked at him and said, what's it good for? That's the question. Maybe it's bad. And when Yoel woke from his nap the novel he wanted to read was lying closed on the table, but his eyes were heavy and the dimness of a Friday evening twilight filled the rooms, and in the stillness of the street the sound of birdsong rose, a twittering voice against a monotonous one, pripipipipi against hoohoohoo. And he closed his eyes and listened a little to this conversation, "conversation" he thought, and suddenly other sounds rose, distant traffic, a guitar being played as it passed behind a wall, and he thought that if only he listened intently he would be able to hear everything, the ants in their cities underneath the building and deep in the earth's crust, and the cats, and the elevators in the luxury towers standing still on their top floors, and the bridges traveling silently through the atmosphere. On the sofa opposite him Emile slept, covered with a thin blanket, a children's book open on his stomach. And Yoel didn't switch the light on so as not to wake Emile, but focused his observation and tried to wipe the webs of sleep from his eyes, after an afternoon nap he always woke up far more tired and heavy than he had been when he went to sleep, and in the faint light coming from the street he looked at Emile for a long time as he slept, and suddenly he felt full of pride at the time that had passed, at the knowledge that even if the world came to an end at that moment, the years that this child had been with him and during which he had given him food and bought him clothes and helped him with his problems and his questions and put money in a savings account for him, damn, the savings account again, why did he always come back to the savings account, it was like a tedious old woman in a felt hat who always turned up at the wrong moment, you again, the savings account, this is your son we're talking about. And he tried to silence the old woman, in other words the savings account, and he said to her, in other words to himself, you talk about him like someone throwing a penny to a poor person, but no, Yoel resisted the nagging voice, you're his father. And he glanced at the book cover and got up to pee, and then he went back and took the book, and opened it in the lavatory and switched on the light and closed his eyes against the sudden glare, and glanced at the text on the back cover as he sat on the lavatory seat and peed, and then he started to read the book itself, suddenly he was full of a passionate desire to read, and he thought that there was nothing better than reading in the lavatory, which was a kind of little reading room where nobody disturbed you and nothing distracted your attention, and he read the first pages of one of the books whose names he had picked up somewhere, a big, that is to say, thick, American novel, he read with concentration, and started to "get into it," to understand what it was about. It's a great thing, reading, he thought, people don't know what they're missing . . . and he passed his finger over the edges of the half-closed book and the paper cut his finger and blood burst from the cut. He stood up and went to the sink, and put the book down for a minute on the washing machine, and left the room. The blood mingled with the water and trickled down the side of the sink. And the child was awake.

They sat down to eat their Friday-night dinner, and the book sat on the corner of the washing machine sometimes until the evening of the next day, and then it went back to its place on the bookshelf until the next Friday came round, and usually until some other Friday weeks later, because the week after Yoel would choose another book to read on Friday afternoon, but the books almost always landed up on the corner of the washing machine, next to the boxes of dental floss and the toothbrushes, including Leah's toothbrush, which Yoel could never bring himself to throw into the trash. Because how, he thought, how? Take it and throw it away? Today of all days throw the toothbrush away? And what then? And for almost twenty years it was stuck there. Until one day it disappeared. And Yoel didn't say a word, even though he was furious. He searched for it all over the house. Under the washing machine. In all the rooms. He climbed ladders. Turned over the mattresses. Banged the cupboards. Rummaged through the cutlery. It didn't do any good. Nothing.

And sometimes he would return to the living room without a book and fall asleep on the sofa like a log for half an hour, and Emile would say to him afterward, when he woke up, "How deeply you slept," and Yoel would deny it, no no, he wasn't sleeping, he just closed his eyes for a minute, he was just thinking about something . . . But the shadows had already settled in the house, and somebody had to get up and switch on the lights, and at a distance of three meters in the living room they looked at each other a few minutes longer, one breathing in and one breathing out, as if there were only one unit of air standing between them, one breath shared between them. And Yoel got up, like a man waking up too late on a train and with his eyes gummed by sleep hurrying to collect his belongings, forgetting his coat hanging on the hook by the window, the scenery outside already moving past, and he walked slowly down the passage, followed by the child who for a minute he had forgotten existed, and he put the salad on the table and cut two slices of exactly the same size from the pea-and-broad-bean pie he made most Fridays because he had read somewhere that green lentils are a good substitute for meat. He would put a Shlomo Artzi disk on the stereo and turn the volume low but not too low, and they would sit down to eat. Yoel stopped chewing and turned to look at the stereo. If there was one song he loved it was "Neriums." And once he sang along with Shlomo

Artzi, on the record that is, and for some reason he burst into bitter tears. And he wanted to write to Shlomo Artzi about this song and he even wrote a long letter that he never sent. The song came closer, he knew exactly when it would arrive. Therefore he swallowed carefully, as though the sound of his swallowing could disturb the music, and Emile felt that he too should stop eating, and that his father expected him to do so, but he was hungry and he piled more salad and more pie onto his plate and chewed the lettuce noisily. Later Emile went out to eat shwarma in the town, and Yoel suddenly said: "And what if I wasn't here."

There were clouds outside the window, yellow and gray and white. The music came to an end and Yoel looked at the stereo for a long time, as if expecting something, and then he looked back at Emile. "Tomorrow I'm going to meet your biological parents," said Yoel, or wanted to say, but saying nothing. "By the sea."

Down below, on the streets of the city, whole families shopped at night. Stores were open. All the streetlights were on. Laden carts. Distant deliveries.

A jay hopped onto the windowsill, and Yoel tilted his head back and thought, "Those pigeons."

[   ]

Once he saw this in a movie. How a man sits facing a wall and a kind of thread comes out of his head and it stops at the wall, but then it goes through it easily, and already it's in the next room, and already it's passing through thicker walls, and going down and passing through the floor, through ceilings and other barriers, and empty open spaces too, tearing clouds and making its way to the sea, coming out dry and again, like a needle through cloth, sewing walls, bulwarks, whole cities vanishing as if they had never existed. And then, far from there, in a strange house, there's a brief ring. And someone goes over, picks up.

He looked at the walls as if he could see through them. Every day he gave him up. Every day. Every day.

In his recurring dream they called and asked: Well, are you coming? And he looked at his watch and saw that he was already a little late.

YOEL

He got out of the taxi at the address given to him by the go-between, 117 Levinsky, with the printout of the email sent to him by Emile's parents in his pocket.

He stood in front of the house. He raised his eyes to the bridge. The bridge he knew very well. The house he didn't remember seeing before.

"Tired of doing odd jobs? Want to show that you're worth more and earn money accordingly? Apply today." "Kingdom of the Fork." "All types of clocks and watches mended. Broken watches. Standing clocks. Pendulum clocks." And over the door of the shop was a big clock with hands forever frozen at five past ten.

Five past ten? Kingdom of the fork? Strange, strange.

He went into the new central bus station. A lot of T-shirts and baked goods for sale. In a bookshop he saw one of the classics of Hebrew literature whose fame had spread far and wide, squashed under a hundred others stacked on the floor. He didn't remember what the book was about, but he was sure that it had some connection to the army, one of the wars, the history of Israel hitherto untold . . . And suddenly, as he was about to bend down to pull the book out, he thought he saw the father passing on level 5, holding a black guitar case in his hand. Yoel went to the shwarma stall. "What do you want on it," they asked him and opened a pita. He didn't hear. He followed the man's receding back. They were already smearing the pita with hummus and filling it with salad. Is it him? Yoel tried to get a better look, but the man was already gone.

He wanted to get out of there. To go to them. But suddenly he realized he should have brought a gift . . . Where were his manners? . . . Turning up at somebody's home for the first time, empty handed?

A gift, a gift. And then he relaxed, he was surrounded by shops. He would find something easily. And he started to look. What could he get them? T-shirts? Hot pies? Perfume, perhaps perfume for the mother? And for the father, Alligator aftershave? No, no, that was too cheap. Everything here was fake. A clock? How about books? Maybe a cake? But that was ridiculous, he thought. A cake, really, how could he bring them a cake? A lamp? A steam iron? A car vacuum cleaner? A salad chopper? A set of knives? Refrigerator magnets? An MP3 player in any one of a selection of colors? His eyes scanned the array of gifts. Propane for their grill? All-purpose detergent? A fur-covered travel mug? A thermometer? One of those executive toys with the four colliding silver balls? I have aromatic oils too . . . how about a giant pop-up lighter?

He went up a few escalators and emerged from another side of the station, next to the line 27 stop. From here the three towers next to his house looked small and remote, as if they were standing in a country very far away. And then a bus moved away, opening up a wider view, and Yoel saw their apartment. He saw the shutters. The upper ramp of the bus station passed a few meters in front of the shuttered window of the third-floor apartment. And he knew with absolute certainty that they lived there. The only window with the shutters closed.

* * *

They sat next to the wooden table that [   ] had made for the child when [   ] was pregnant. And sometimes they stumbled on its miniature chairs and she said to him, enough, throw them out, they're in the way, I've got bruises all over my leg from them, it's enough. As if somebody had taken stray dogs in from the street only to have their ankles bitten.

The gift lay in its wrapping on a kind of shelf. Yoel leaned against the shutters. "I don't understand why you ran away from me at the seaside. How could you run away like that?"

A cat suddenly appeared next to his leg, pressed up against him. And he wanted to ask them: What's its name, this cat?

* * *

Yoel thought about how one day Emile would enter this apartment and walk down the hall where the pictures he would give them and they would enlarge until they were almost blurred would be hanging, and with every step he would pass by his life, the park, the flower beds, the Ferris wheel, the things that made up his memories, and go into the empty living room, and there would be a dark green tree in the window, next to a very ugly neon-lit bridge abutment, and the sun would come into the window and draw two rectangles on a white wall, and that enormous old sewing machine would stand there as if speaking. This what a room looks like with nobody in it and nobody looking at it. And Emile would see the sunlight lying on the walls, and he would look at his little bed, a bed he had never slept in because they gave him up at the hospital and never brought him home, and the bed remained in the living room for a year, two years, for seven years until she said, burn it, give it to the children to burn in their bonfire, and he said, I'll burn it, I'll give it to the children to burn in a bonfire, but he pushed it into the storeroom instead, and there it lay for almost forty years and only the dust slept on it in the afternoons. The rectangles of light would disappear, the tree would sway in the wind, buses would drive noisily over the bridge, climbing to their last stop, and Emile would sit on the bed and then he would lie down and go to sleep on it. But it wouldn't happen.

* * *

Yoel noticed, in the next room, a black oud case lying face down under an empty bookcase.

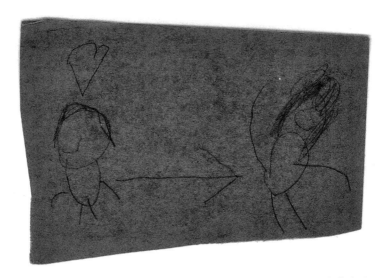

At the age of five Emile drew this and said to him, to Yoel, "It's for him" and Yoel "didn't understand" who "him" was and so didn't react. And then he asked, "Who's him?" and Emile said, "Him, the real one," and Yoel told himself on no account could he show that he was hurt, never mind angry, and he said to Emile, "It's very good that you love him too, he's your father too, no two ways about it," and Emile said, "No, just him, just him, his name is Danny," and Yoel said, "I am too, I am too, Emile," and Emile said, "You don't look like me at all, everybody says so." And Yoel reached out and snatched the drawing that over the years faded and blurred until it turned into what he called "the cave painting." But he didn't have the heart to throw it away. He put the picture down next to the plate of cookies and the water and stood up quickly, mumbling, "This is for you."

And a voice rose from the other end of the room and asked if it was possible to use the bathroom. They pointed with their chins. Yoel went out into the hallway. They looked at each other without saying a word. The hallway was empty, as if they'd just moved in, or were just about to move out, after packing up all their belongings and sending them on ahead, and so you stand there for a couple of minutes and look at this house which reveals all its cracks to you and all the dirt that's lain for years behind closets and sofas eating away at their bones. Yoel opened a door. It was their bedroom. He saw an iron bed and a mattress without a sheet and a flat, thin pillow fastened shut with three buttons.

He couldn't remember what he'd bought them.

He wanted to go back into the main hallway and find the bathroom, which he now needed urgently, but in the place where he remembered the door leading to a room with chairs and newspapers, there was an open closet. He soon realized that the closet was not in fact a solid obstruction and he dried his sweat and walked through the door and straight out again through the door on the other side, it was a kind of two-sided closet, finding himself on a porch full of junk.

From another, parallel passage they called him.

Many years ago he hid from Yoel and Leah. "Emile, Emile," they called him. At first they laughed, but the child didn't want to be found. Or he did want to, but he also wanted to run away. They searched the whole house but they couldn't find him, they opened the doors, and they began to sweat, they began to shout, and their upstairs neighbor came down and she began to help them search, and another neighbor came down with a broom, he thought the cat had got in from the yard again and they couldn't find it. He had hidden himself very well. Yes, he knew how to disappear. Did you look in the kitchen cupboards? And they hurried to the kitchen cupboards, and lined up in a row, and then they opened the doors. But he wasn't there either.

Yoel went back into the living room. The mother and her eyes were sitting there, in the same place. The little picture was lying on the table, face down. The cookies were glum and mute. The tea was lukewarm and bitter. She hadn't sweetened it for him, just as she never sweetened it for her husband. Buses drove past all the time on the bridge.

And they knew, now there was supposed to be a great talk. But they couldn't say a word. There was a kind of fatigue. Paralysis took hold. Like opening a window in the afternoon and outside it's completely dark, and you look around, is it a dream, and you don't see the children in the street looking through smoked glass at the sun eclipsed by the moon. You don't understand and you don't know what to do. What to say.

So he sat there facing them in their apartment in silence, until they asked to speak to each other for a few minutes alone, if he was willing to go and wait in the next room. The room next door. If he could just give them five minutes.

He glanced at the gift. They hadn't touched it. But it seemed to have aged now, all the splendor of the wrapping had vanished. Or it was the light that had faded.

And Yoel said that it didn't matter, that he gave up, that he understood them, that the whole idea didn't make any sense to begin with, and bursting in on them like this without prior warning, no no, he hadn't received any email from them, very strange, that they seemed like good people, that he wanted to leave now, to go already, what's the time, I want to sleep. And he thought that he would go to the bus station, buy himself a cheap pasty and a cold drink, that he would eat meat after thirty years of strict vegetarianism. Shwarma and hamburgers. He would eat meat. Put on fat. Today I want chops.

But the mother put her hand on the drawing and said, five minutes? And Yoel bowed his head and walked out. He thought of how he would go into the next room and find a child there, bump into him, a very thin kind of child, like a carpet, he treads on him without noticing, the child doesn't react, look, it's Emile, what are you doing here, but no, it turns out that they had another child a year later. And the child is lying on straw, chained to the wall.

He stood in the next room with his face to the wall. His nose touched the windowsill. His lips touched the plaster. Apparently he was talking to the wall. The words seeped in. Yes, he would come back and bring her all the clothes, he promised the wall. He would come and bring her all the clothes. Which he had kept. In a bag. In bags. In the closet. The dress. And the hat. All her towels.

The bras.

The parents had been watching him for some time in silence.

The three of them returned to the living room, in a long, humiliated convoy. What was the time?

Look, they said to him, we've decided to explain it to you. Because otherwise you'll never leave us alone, they thought. You're part of it. You put in a lot of effort. "And your wife!" And [   ] said: A few days before we met you that first time by the sea we sat here, and we said to ourselves . . . and the father intervened: We're being evicted. "You're being evicted," repeated Yoel. They're going to destroy the building, to expand the central bus station, to add a light-rail station, an elevated train. "Like in Chicago." Engineers from Chicago came to see us. They drank water from the glass you're drinking from now. There'll be another commercial floor added to the station too, a shopping mall. There's a plan, the City Planning and Construction Committee approved the plan. The exterior bridge will become an interior bridge, they'll install an escalator on it. The City Planning and Construction Committee, said Yoel uncomprehendingly. We submitted our objections, our objections were overruled, said the mother. They're going to evict us, but we won't leave. What do you mean you won't leave. Of course we'll leave, she said, I'm just telling you what we said then, a few days before we met you on the beach. What did you say? That we won't leave. Really, said Yoel. You won't leave, and then they'll bring in bulldozers and flatten the building. What do you mean, you won't leave? And [   ] said: We said to ourselves, we'll hide here, there's a room where the guy who did the renovations used to put things, it's got a two-sided closet, we said: we'll come at night, we'll sit in the closet. Two-sided, eh, you'll sit in the closet, Yoel repeated like an idiot. Yes, in the closet, we'll sit in the closet. And what then? demanded Yoel, and turned his hand palm up. They demolish the building and it collapses on top of the closet. And you? Yoel laughed like a moron. Buried alive! announced [   ] and slapped his knee. Together, added his wife. What's the point, asked Yoel. He had nothing to say. What's the point? she repeated, the point is to die. To die in the closet, explained [   ], that was the idea. To die for urban reconstruction, laughed Yoel. They averted their eyes and looked at the bridge. What's the connection, though . . . that's not what I asked, is it? The one thing's got nothing to do with the other, he wanted to say.

But in the end we decided not to do it, she said, as if to reassure him.

In his dream, that morning, he stretched out his hands like a blind man who's sensed something close to him, rearing his head back and to the side, turning an ear to the light he couldn't see, his fingers almost extending out of his hand. Now he remembered it. And the father said to Yoel, in yesterday's dream, in which they were still on the sand by the sea: You want us to show you his bed? It's in the storeroom. I can go up and bring it down to you. If you like I'll go up now and bring the bed down. As far as I'm concerned, you can have it. And the mother shouted in the distance, No, no, don't give him the bed. And she held on to the blanket.

And Yoel turned to them and said quietly, no, no . . . you don't understand, you don't understand . . . let me explain to you, you don't understand what's going on here . . . you sit here without saying anything, it's all up to me . . . and then his voice suddenly hardened and rose, maybe I didn't make myself clear, I insist, I insist, you can't expect, you can't expect that because of that . . . I understand, I understand your distress . . . but it's not . . . that's not it . . . I didn't explain, I'll explain to you again, you have to take . . . Why don't you say anything, he yelled, why do you keep quiet, don't you understand Hebrew. And suddenly he lifted his head, fixed his eyes on them, and took two or three steps toward the parents, who stood there, not knowing what to do with him, he went up to [   ] and took hold of him with both hands, he held his shoulders hard and yelled, all I'm asking of you, and he felt an overwhelming desire to crush him, we, we have . . . the wife was still holding her husband's arm, and Yoel stood in front of him and held him with both hands and shook him hard, and she put out her hand to Yoel's chest and tried to push him away from her husband, who stood there without reacting, as if he had fallen asleep standing up, staring into space, and Yoel said, I insist, I'm not letting you off so easily, you have obligations too, we, and she tried to push him away but she couldn't do it with one hand, and Yoel didn't even feel the hand pressing on his ribs, his fingers were now digging into the shoulders of the staring [   ], gripping him, why didn't they want to, why were they saying no without any explanation, everyone says no to me, how about saying "yes" for a change, we, no, I want to say, I'm not letting you off, you

77

won't kick me out, what is this, "no, no," and then your "sorry, it isn't so simple," I insist, I'm still alive, they haven't buried me yet, you're not going to kick me out again, you hear? Not again, no, what is this, running away like that, I won't allow it, I won't allow it, I'm the father of this child, are you listening to me at all? Are you listening to me or not? Let me talk to you, you'll let me talk, and all of a sudden he let go of [   ]'s shoulders, and the wife's hand sent him flying. He stumbled and hit the shutter and sat on the floor under the window.

[   ] went on standing there, his hands hanging at his sides.

And half an hour later the three of them were still sitting there. They on chairs, he on the floor in the corner to which he had been pushed. He couldn't see so well anymore. He covered his face. He didn't think he would ever be able to get up again. All the strength had left his body. [   ] walked out backward and returned with a folded winter blanket in his hands.

Don't be angry with us, Yoel, they said to him. We thought it was clear to you. That it's him, it's **him** who doesn't want us, she whispered. You know yourself that by law from the age of eighteen the file can be opened . . . they call it "unification." And nearly twenty years have passed and he hasn't come. We thought he would come already in '88, we marked the date on the calendar . . . we put a circle round it . . .

He doesn't need us . . .

Did you ask the child before you came to talk to us? You didn't ask him. You yourself said, on the beach, that you didn't. You said he didn't know anything. You . . . isn't it clear to you? The child doesn't want us. He's already been telling us for nearly twenty years, every day . . . Why can't you understand? And Yoel raised his eyes to theirs.

*　*　*

And finally he dragged his feet from one end of the room to the other, without saying a word, hunched over, holding the hem of the checked blanket draped round his shoulders. And [　　] followed him and locked the door behind him, peering at his back through the murky peephole and turning the key slowly so he wouldn't hear. And while [　　] was leaning over, watching that blurred spot receding down the corridor, he thought that if only he had asked the first question, all the questions after it would have flowed of their own accord. He had a lot of questions and once he'd even thought of writing them down. A notebook of questions. To ask Yoel about the years. How they'd gone by. No no, not every minute, not every week, but only the outlines . . . As a baby. As a child. As a boy. An adolescent. Did he have a hard time living. When did they tell him that he was, well, "adopted." How did he react. Was he angry. Was he still angry. What did Yoel and Leah tell him about them. How did they explain to him. Were there any children. That is, do we have grandchildren whose names we don't even kno. And more. And more. And more and more. But his eye was now completely closed behind the peephole, and Yoel had disappeared long ago around the bend in the corridor. When [   ] looked back into the room, his wife wasn't there anymore either. He was alone. And all this time two of his fingers had been holding the key stuck in the keyhole, one finger on each side.

And Yoel stopped at the end of the corridor and turned back. A kind of half turn. If only they'd said half a word, if only they would turn to him even now and ask him, even here, even from the door in the distance, if it opened for a minute, he would shout to them, maybe being close like that was hard for them, I understand, he would tell them everything from the end of the corridor, he wouldn't hide anything from them. My memories are yours, he wanted to say to them, I'm so glad you asked, I remember that perfectly . . . And he would tell them everything, honestly, albeit in digest form, everything, but without hurting them, he would leave out what didn't need to be said. Don't be afraid, he would shout to them, and they would crowd in the doorway that they would open to him in the end, we have to leave it all behind us, he wanted to say, and then he said, in the corridor, looking at the closed door, he shouted, we have to leave it all behind us. And a terrible kind of grin spread over his face, until he turned away, walking backward, until he left the dirty peephole behind.

Yoel went downstairs, this time in an elevator he discovered there, a freight elevator at the back of the building. There was a strong smell of oranges in the elevator, and he went down in it, sitting on a big, low box. The birds flew in the tops of the orange trees, and she opened the curtain a little way and a soft gray light filtered in, more like illuminated darkness than light, and it fell on Yoel's face too as he gradually awakened, as if a new sun was rising inside him. It wasn't even six in the morning, and she said, half to him and half in a whisper, what she said then, that morning, Those birds, it's like waking up in the stock exchange. What a noise. And that smell all the time, what is this place, an orange grove? I'll go and see what's happening with our apartment in the new building, it's past time we moved out of here already, and Emile wants to as well. I'll go and check what's happening, how about you make a change and come with me? But Yoel didn't want to hear about it now, Emile wants to, what did Emile have to do with it. She dragged Emile into everything. He heard the birds chirping and without a doubt talking to each other, answering one another, and there was a meaning to this chatter, no, it wasn't music but actual speech, a peep here and then a peep in response. I'll go to a bookshop and look for books about the language of the birds, he thought, it's clear that they're saying something, and he wanted to get out of bed and go over to Leah, put his hands on her shoulders, but he didn't get up, he closed his eyes and went back to sleep, and Leah got ready and woke Emile and took him to school as she did every morning, and when Yoel woke up it was already broad daylight and hot, and the curtain was drawn, flapping against the windowpane, and her half cup of black coffee was still warm on the table and he took a sip of it as usual, and the phone rang and rang, and he didn't answer it, but it didn't stop ringing until he picked it up and said, yes, who the hell is it at this hour of the morning. And a very quiet, almost inaudible voice informed him. And then silence fell. And for a long time he stood there empty. Until he blinked and the elevator crashed into his mind like a heavy, rusty freight car, rushing down the shaft like a perpendicular underground train carrying a single passenger. He didn't take in what had been said to him, but after a second he was forced to take it in, all at once, as if someone was forcing his jaws open and pouring poison down his throat, the sight of his wife pressing and pressing the red "stop" button in the new building as soon as she realized that something had gone wrong, and something really had gone wrong, and she huddled into the corner of the racing plunging hurtling cubicle and prayed for a miracle, for a sudden halt, and thought about Emile and the sky-blue schoolbag she had bought him only two months ago, in honor of his first year at school, and only an hour ago she had looked at him quickly, and then at the schoolbag in the sunlight, no, no, help, he shouted, shouted out loud, help, stop. And wrapped in the blanket he emerged into the street.

II

THE CITY

Between two endless ice ages the city sprouted like a patch of moss on a wall in a godforsaken neighborhood. And it was hot in the city, and people sweated, and they ate yellow popsicles, frozen lemon, sweet under a pleasant winter sun. And the ice cubes lay in the fridge, small and square, like bricks in a house that would never be built. But before it and behind it the big ice loomed, like a pair of snowy brackets. He put the sleeping feverish child down on the bed. On her side. He went to the fridge, opened the freezer, and put his head inside it.

LEAH–YOEL

To tell the truth they had made up their minds to choose a girl, but there were a lot more boys, and none of the girls appealed to Leah. Yoel was impatient, just like a man with his wife in a dress shop. Every second in the ward of children available for adoption oppressed him and shamed him as if he wasn't adopting a child but committing a serious crime in broad daylight, and he said, speaking to the floor, after a couple of minutes, "Come on, it's enough already," and Leah said, "Yoel, this isn't a dress shop, you can't bring it back it if doesn't fit. What's the matter with you? Have a little patience," and she smiled apologetically at the nurse. Then she pointed to a red-haired baby girl and looked at Yoel for approval, and he said, "Okay, let's take the ginger one. My mother was a redhead too. It works," and they picked up the baby, who was very light, frighteningly light, Yoel recalled, and Leah thought, "That's all I need, his mother." His hands had been ready for a heavy burden, and the burden was light, and he said, "Great, can we go now?" And Leah said, "Yes, I always wanted a ginger daughter," and Yoel said, "But won't she get burned in the summer? Her skin's sensitive . . . My mother had freckles all over," and he touched his mother's smooth arm. And Leah said, suppressing her annoyance, "What do you want? We've already chosen, you want to give her back now?" and she said to the nurse, who stood waiting on one side, stretching a black rubber ring between her fingers, making strange, complicated shapes with it, squares and ellipses, "Right, we've chosen this one," and the nurse began to laugh. The nurse, who was a redhead too, started laughing and coughing, and after she calmed down she said that the baby they'd chosen was her baby, the nurse's baby, I keep her here so I don't have to pay for a babysitter, what's the matter with you, couldn't you see she was a baby with a mother? And Yoel said, "Sorry, we didn't realize," and the nurse said, "Never mind, I take it as a compliment," and Leah said, "Okay, so we'll take the one next to her," and she pointed at the bed to the right of the one where the red-headed baby had been immediately returned, and the nurse said, "No problem, you've got it, come back tomorrow to fill in the forms," and Yoel was disappointed, what, can't we take her now? And he picked up the baby with the black hair, who turned out to be a boy.

YOEL

And sometimes he thought, just before he closed his eyes, I forgot to water the plants. The soil in the planters was hot and dry. And with his eyes half closed he would get up and take a glass, fill it, and asleep on his feet he would water the plants. Drink, drink. Going from room to room. Reaching with his fingers to switch off the light. Touching the wall. A little moonlight spilled in from the street. On the shelf the candlesticks glittered and likewise the gilt letters on the covers of the volumes of the dictionary and the galaxy on the cover of the astronomy book for children he had bought for Emile. Sometimes after an hour or two he woke up. The absolute silence. The child wrapped in blankets. The glasses lying on the table. Her bowls in the dark, in the kitchen. And the moon that had risen fully and steadied itself in the meantime. In the cupboard. One o'clock at night. To go back to sleep or stay up till morning. And "Leah? Leah?" And he drinks. Falls asleep sitting up. And he wakes up and doesn't understand what he's doing there at this hour of night.

And Emile didn't know that he was still awake, looking at him. And once Yoel, who had been sitting for a long time watching the sleeping child, was startled to hear, "I haven't got a father," and he couldn't bear it, and he fell onto his bed, his nose in the pillow.

The next morning Emile lay sprawled over the big double bed, whereas Yoel woke up in Emile's bed, curled up and frozen and covered only to his waist. And there was no knowing what had happened that night to bring them to this pass.

YOEL–EMILE

On the morning of the day after the funeral he told Emile about the angels that would watch over her. "Up there . . . above the clouds," he said. "And it isn't hot there and it isn't cold," he said. And Emile sat down and drew one of them, the one in the hat. "Is that God?" "No, it's an angel." "An angel?" "The Angel of Death."— "What?"

A month later Yoel called in some movers to take away the double bed. The angel with the skinny legs looked down from the wall at the mattress being dragged out of the room. In its place he put a twin-sized mattress and carried it up to the apartment himself. The mattress, struggling through the bends in the narrow passage of the stairwell, getting slammed and stuck and bent out of shape, groaned as if it just wanted to go back home to Sleep and Furniture World on Rosh Pina Street. Yoel went up to the linen cupboard but all the bed linen was for a double bed. At first he put the sheets on the mattress and tried to fold them over, but the results were appalling, the sheets trailed along the floor as if they had been spilled there. He tried to push the sheet underneath the mattress, but it only made things worse. No, he thought, and pulled the sheet off by force, no. He lay down on the bare mattress and said to himself, I'll sleep like this. Without a sheet, without a pillow. I'll sleep rough. His fingers ran over the surface of the new mattress. He could feel the springs.

That same morning Shula, his mother, called. He heard his father whispering, telling her what to say. "Does he need anything? The most important thing is to start living again. We know this matchmaker, she's been successful in plenty of difficult cases . . . You remember our neighbor, the widow . . . It's been a month already, the main thing is not to sink . . . " And Yoel said, "What, what, I can't hear you, there are problems with the line," and put the phone down.

Yoel lay down. A few days before, at Sleep and Furniture World, the salesman had said to him, "You need a mattress for a son? A daughter?" and Yoel said, with suppressed anger, "No, for myself," and the salesman said, "Then you shouldn't be looking at the juvenile sizes." And Yoel retreated to the adult department, but there were only double beds there, and he wanted to ask the salesman what a man like him was supposed to do, he didn't dare utter the word "widower" even in his thoughts, which is to say that he began to utter and then quashed it. Why do you assume that from a certain age a person must be part of a couple and so sleep on a double bed, always buy two movie tickets and two plane tickets, get charged for two in every hotel room, is given a table for two, a two-seated bicycle. These and other images came into Yoel's head as he lay on the demonstration mattress in the shop, stretching his legs in order to feel, in the words of the salesman, "how comfortable it is." And he knew that this situation was humiliating, shameful. He was like someone who had lost his wallet and was running around, anguished, and in order to explain to people why he's so upset he just keeps repeating "I lost my wallet, I lost my wallet!" and no one believes him, they think he's crazy, what wallet.

Suddenly he jumped. Hands had started to massage his stocking feet, and he sat up on the bed and saw a Chinese saleslady bending over his feet, and he said, what's this, what's going on here, but the salesman reassured him, reflexology, relax, you'll see how good it is, your whole body is there on the sole of your foot, she'll open up your meridians, nobody knows about it here in Israel, we brought her specially from China, by train . . . And Yoel, who on the one hand was embarrassed to the depths of his soul, and on the other suddenly felt the acute pleasure of a foot getting its very first massage, said, no need, no need, and the salesman said, signaling to the woman to carry on and saying a few words in Chinese, yes, she'll stop in a minute, it's on the house, the lady came specially all the way from China, it took her a month to get here, don't insult her, she'll take it hard, very hard, and he added a few more words in Chinese, and you're under no obligation to buy a mattress from me just because . . .

The double mattress on display at Sleep and Furniture World was indeed very comfortable, Yoel had never slept on such a comfortable mattress in his life, so firm and supportive, until all he wanted at that moment was to close his eyes and go to sleep, and with every compression of the points of pleasure or pleasurable pain on the sole of his foot he sank a little deeper, as if he were floating in the minute gap between sleep and wakefulness, in a kind of fluffy gray cotton, inside a cloud. He still heard the salesman saying, "You want to sleep, eh? You want me to put a pillow under your head, take a half hour nap?" and when Yoel didn't answer, he felt strong fingers raising his neck and pushing a pillow under his head. The pillow astonished him, because all his life he had only ever had a thin, flat pillow covered with brown stains that for years had twisted his neck, a pillow more like a little folded blanket than a pillow, and here was something new, a comfortable pillow, comfortable wasn't the word, thick, supporting the head and neck, thick but without the head sinking into it, springy but supporting the nape of the neck, and the mattress was a perfect match for the pillow, supporting his whole tired body, which was yearning for sleep after a hard day's work, sweet is the sleep of the laborer, ha ha, it was ten past nine in the morning. And all at once Yoel sank into sleep. Not before thinking, You shouldn't have shaved, everyone will think that nothing's wrong. Instead of going to the grave you're going to sleep. And before he went to sleep he also thought about how his mother could come into the shop and find him lying there. And a dream rose from the mattress and the pillow and his feet and filled him, and in the dream he and Leah were lying on the old bed and Emile was lying between them, even though the psychologist from the adoption services had warned them not to let the child sleep in their bed. But they paid no attention to this warning, and Emile slept between them almost every

94

night, until one night, at the age of four or five, he got up in his sleep and floated through the darkness of the apartment to his own bed and went on sleeping there and never came back. And it took a few days for them to notice that he wasn't there.

In his furniture shop dream Yoel got up after Emile and followed him silently in the night and saw how he, the little Emile, paused next to the brown chest of drawers and took out a comb and stood there combing his hair in his sleep, looking in the little mirror with his eyes closed and combing his hair, and Yoel stood there in dismay and didn't know what to do. Whether to take the comb out of his hand and startle him, but on the other hand, perhaps there was a danger that he might comb his eyes and blind himself, thought Yoel in his dream, and he went back to the bedroom to ask Leah what to do, as he always asked her, even about less serious matters ("What should I give him for supper?" "Cucumber or tomato?" "Tell me, does he like butter?" and one time he cut Emile's hair himself, and it came out a mess, and the next morning they presented themselves at Levy's barbershop, hats on both their heads), and he stood in the bedroom doorway and whispered in order to wake her up and ask her, until he saw, in the darkness of three o'clock in the morning, that in the place where the double bed should have been there was a huge pit, like an excavation at a building site. Far below the building workers were laying the foundations, and in the center of the pit Yoel made out an iron pole and he reached out his hand, and although the pole was far away his fingers touched it. When he opened his eyes the staff of the furniture shop were standing round him, the salesman and the Chinese reflexologist and a few others, with gratified expressions on their faces. Sir, we're delighted, the salesman rubbed his hands together, soft and plump as pillows, you fell asleep, eh? Fast asleep! So allow me to inform you that our store's policy entitles you to a further ten percent reduction in addition to the twenty percent of the sale, and what's more, the pillow, sir, the pillow! It's yours, as a gift. Fast asleep! Nine in the morning and he falls asleep, nine in the morning and he's already tired, the dear man! And the entire staff applauded. But Yoel stood up in embarrassment and apologized, "No, no, I just nodded off," and the salesman chortled, beaming with joy, "If you call **that** nodding off! If you call **that** nodding off!" And Yoel said to himself, "I dreamed a dream," but the salesman didn't hear him, "I don't understand, don't you want the discount?" and Yoel said, "I don't know, I just dozed off for a minute," and the salesman asked, "Did you dream? That's what counts. Did you dream or not?" The Chinese woman said something in Chinese and the salesman nodded vigorously. And Yoel, who was suddenly overwhelmed, said in a tone of alarm, staring at the salesman, "I had a nightmare," and sat down on the bed. The salesman said, "That's not news to me. When people are so comfortable . . . " And he nodded sadly. "We had a customer once, an officer high-up in the army, he fell asleep here and dreamed that war broke out. He woke up sobbing like a baby. We didn't know what to say to him. If I told you his name you'd faint dead away." From somewhere or other a cup of tea and Petit Beurre biscuit were produced and handed to Yoel. The sales assistants stared in silence, their heads slightly bowed. Yoel took a few sips of tea and stood up and said, "I'll take one like that, but single," but the salesman said, "I'm sorry, it doesn't come in a single. It only comes in a double, I can't saw it in half," and Yoel looked around himself like a person lost in a dense forest of beds and mattresses and then pointed at random at a single mattress leaned up against a corner and said, "Then I'll take that one," and he added, "and give me the pillow too, in fact I'll have two of them." Only then he saw that they had taken off his socks when he was sleeping, and replaced them with clean white socks. "Naughty socks," he said to the salesman, who replied, "Of course, of course."

A few hours after his new mattress had been placed on the floor of the bedroom, which had suddenly grown very big and empty, Yoel collected all the double sheets and took them down to the bench in the avenue. One of his neighbors, a divorcee, looked at him and thought, "Throwing away his sheets, really, what on earth does he think he's doing." And that night he couldn't sleep. The touch of the new, bare mattress was as unpleasant as lying on a rough road. The angel looked out from its wall to the opposite wall and laughed. It's like sleeping on a bed of nails, Yoel thought, like sleeping on sand, like sleeping on cold asphalt. And he got up in the middle of the night and went to the top half of the closet and in a grumpy half sleep pulled down one of the sheets Emile had received for his birthday from Yoel's parents, with pictures of Darth Vader and Luke Skywalker and Han Solo with laser guns printed on it, and he threw the sheet onto the mattress and sleepily crammed his new pillow into the matching pillowcase with the two crossed swords of light and fell asleep. When he woke up in the morning Emile was close to him on the narrow mattress, asleep on comets and suns.

They woke up late. Yoel's parents had turned up first thing, at a quarter to six they were already there, knocking and ringing, but father and son didn't hear them and so didn't let them in. And the lock had been changed long ago, in vain did they try to insert their key and turn it. And Emile sat on the new mattress and asked Yoel, before they got up, all the questions, one after the other. All of a sudden. Out of the blue. Who were his parents and what were their names. Where did they live. And why did they abandon him. And did he really have eight grandmothers and grandfathers like the children in his class said when they teased him. And why didn't they come now. And why did Mommy go into the broken elevator. And if people who died came back afterward to visit their children. And whether it was possible that all this was just a dream and they would wake up in a little while and laugh. And why God didn't send two angels to stop the fall like in the bible. And anyway, what kind of a name was "Emile," did his birth parents give him this name to insult him, or so that they would be able to recognize him easily later on, when they came to look for him. And also: "How much did you pay for me?"

Yoel listened to the questions. He couldn't look at Emile. And so he fixed his eyes on the door.

And that evening, when he got up to leave the room and switch off the light, Emile clung to his hand and said to him in the dark, "I love you more than Mommy." And Yoel leaned for a minute against the door frame, his forehead hot, his arm stretched out in front of him, and when he got his breath back he said to Emile, "Why, why, there's no need for more, less," and Emile said, "It's because you're bringing me up."

[   ]

On the wall of the central bus station synagogue someone had
pasted a page printed with the words: "Pray for the child Hannah
Bilha Fichman laid low by suffering in need of help." He passed
there every day and didn't see the page. And then one day he saw
it. He knew the name. He didn't know from where. And he wanted
to pray but he didn't know what to say. So he simply said her name
once and then once again. And again an inner voice told him that
he knew her. That he had heard her name. That he had read about
her in the newspaper. A complicated operation. Request for do-
nations. Famous doctor from abroad. Organ donation. Suddenly
he had the feeling that she was no longer among the living, that
any prayers were already moot. That he had already seen this sign
years ago, that he just hadn't read about it. They'd gone on sticking
them up for no reason. The charity had been exposed as fictitious,
there was no such child. Unless that was a different case? And he
remembered her, that little girl, later on, when he stood by the sea,
where he went almost every day. It was a hard winter, his umbrella

had been turned inside out and then suddenly carried off toward the city. He stood and hid behind the lifeguard's hut, soon he was soaked through. And he wanted to pray, but he didn't know what to do, he was afraid to do it out loud, nobody had taught him how. And then he tried in a low voice, and nobody heard him, because there was nobody there, he murmured a few sentences to the rain, phrases like "let her be cured," the winter wind will help her, he thought, and he pronounced the ineffable name of God, more than that he did not know, he thought of it spread out in big white letters over the gray waves. Y-A-H-W-E-H, he thought, the wind will come from the sea, it will find the little girl, a saltwater wind, salt disinfects wounds. Amen.

The next day, again, when he came home from the sea, half of him soaked, a new mourning notice was pasted up, covering the earlier page. And he tried to remember the sick child's name, but he was unable to do so.

EMILE

Two months later Emile came home from school with a drawing, "I and my body" in a cardboard folder. It showed a child's body and inside the body was a smaller body (there was also a green sun, and a black fish swimming in the air). And Yoel thought: It's only a print on the shirt in the picture. Yoel thought: It's a mistake, he drew the small figure first and then he drew a bigger one around it. Yoel thought: It's an addition by another child in the class. Look, the child inside is completely different from the one outside. Yoel thought: "Nonsense."

Only many years later, when the drawing had long since disappeared into the folder where Yoel kept all of Emile's drawings, he understood that he'd been wrong. That it was her. Cut out of him. The figure inside the body didn't have eyes or a face. Yoel remembered it very well. One arm too short. The head crooked, a kind of antenna. And then he forgot it again. Until a few days later, standing and shaving in front of the concave mirror, he realized that the little figure was also himself. The razor ran over Yoel's chin, cutting down the stubble. Emile looks at me and sees them. I'm only a superfluous subdivision. That's all. A reminder of something that isn't there. And what isn't there is bigger than the little that is. I'm the little that's there. I'm the little that's there. All his illnesses he got from them. And what from me? Nothing.

He went to the folder to find the drawing and destroy it. But he couldn't find it anywhere.

YOEL–EMILE

And he got up, grabbed his glasses, and ran unshaved to the school, and asked the children in the schoolyard at break, Emile, do you know Emile, and a little girl said, that depends, Emile Cohen, Emile Ben-Naftali, or Emile Zisu, and Yoel latched onto the last and said, that's it, that's it, Zisu, Zisu, and asked, did he come to school today? And the little girl said, ummmm . . . I don't think so, I didn't see him today at all. And Yoel's heart pumped blood and he was sweating and a terrible pressure opened up inside him and he asked, Are you in his class? And she said, I sit next to him, and Yoel began to shiver and shake, and he hung onto the school fence, and the little girl laughed because she thought he was putting on an act for her, and she split her sides laughing and said merrily, I fooled you, I fooled you, he's here, there he is, next to the water fountain, look.

The water fountain wasn't far. Cold water was locked in its pipes. Sparrows drank from the little pool and puffed up their feathers.

The distance could be crossed in a minute. Emile raised his eyes and understood everything immediately.

The school bell rang, the break was over, pigeons flew to their perches. The older kids streamed by. Emile pushed against the stream of children. Yoel wanted to say to him, Don't cry, don't cry. She wasn't really your mother. Because again and again he tried to console himself with this, that the tragedy was his alone, that Leah wasn't, that Leah wasn't, but he was unable to complete the sentence. Because she was, she was. Of course she was. But now, nevertheless, he wanted to say to him, She was only your adoptive mother, now we'll find the mother who gave birth to you and everything will be all right, okay?

But he couldn't say it. Because if **she** isn't neither am I. And if I'm not, the child is completely alone. These thoughts milled round in Yoel's head and took him over completely. He thought of nothing else. Because the fact that Emile had first been given up and now been orphaned into the bargain outraged him. It isn't fair, he wanted to shout, to say to the child, but no. You can't say it. It would only confuse him more. Tell him and be done with it.

He couldn't move.

"Mommy . . . " he said. Withdrew a little from the embrace. "Listen, I . . . something bad happened . . . "

"She's already in the cemetery."
    No, no . . . "

And they left the schoolyard. They opened the small gate for them. A little way off they heard the voice of the Torah teacher, holding a lunch box and the Book of Genesis and bounding toward them. Yoel explained the situation in a lowered voice. He was taking the child home. And would he tell the principal. The Torah teacher tore Yoel's shirt and Emile looked at the white manicured fingers ripping the cloth. Yoel pushed him away with both hands, no, stop it, let go of me. Let go . . .

Behind his back Emile tried to tear his own shirt. But he was too weak.

The father and son walked up the street leading from the school to their house. They stopped at the pedestrian crossing. Passing cars wouldn't let them cross. The traffic was heavy on this street.

And Yoel thought, perhaps we should throw ourselves under the wheels, get run over.

They sat down on a bench in the avenue. Yoel said, "There was apparently an accident in the new building, where we were supposed to move, remember? Mommy went there to see how they were getting on with the construction."

Yoel let Emile dig his teeth into him. Everybody saw and nobody said anything.

And afterward they both dragged their feet in the shade of the trees, and on the stairs Yoel picked Emile up and carried him as he'd done when he was a baby, when they brought him home from the adoption agency and for many days afterward. And he apparently fell asleep in the stairwell, and Yoel put him down on her side of the bed and sat on the floor next to him, and then he stood up and disconnected the telephone so it wouldn't wake him, and sat down again, and looked at the wound and licked it. He didn't know what to do, his head was burning, he didn't have a clue as to what came next, how he would live his life from now on, he was only forty after all, and how was he going to live even today, who was going to cook for the child, and how was he going to miss work the next day. **They won't believe you**, the absurd thought crossed his mind, they'll think you're shirking and fire you, in a minute they'll start wondering where you are and then they'll kick you out, but you have to work to take care of him, you can't afford to lose your job on any account, and then suddenly the rage, which would strike him many more times in the coming weeks, what an idiot, to get into an elevator in an unfinished building, idiot, idiot, stupid fool, and immediately after that the rage at himself for blaming her, why didn't you tell her, why didn't you warn her, and the desire to smash things up, to break the windows, and again the terrible pain, and again the tears, and again the rage, how could you leave me alone with a six-year-old child, and again, immediately, the distress, I'll take care of you, don't worry, and for a moment another voice steals into the grief, it will pass, as if someone from the future is telling him, it will pass, and it has passed, and again he weeps, he screams at the voice, how will it pass, no, no, it will always be here, always, always.

And broken thoughts come into his head, running round, connected and unconnected, an iron knife, a car race, the chariots of Pharaoh, the King of Assyria, a leather sandal, mighty waters, and something like a knife cleaves his heart and he wants to shout, no, no, but the child is still asleep so he doesn't shout yet, he swallows the voice, how can such a thing happen, into the elevator, into the elevator, into the accursed elevator, into the elevator, his soul sinks eight stories into the earth, pulling and pulling, how will it end, into, and again the words hit him, what, what will happen now, he looks at the date, the fourth of the month, and the date seems alien and threatening, and the number four on the calendar seems to be colored red, and it really is colored red, I'm lost, he says, I'm lost, we're lost. And when he woke from his sleep Emile was already bending over his little desk, silently drawing a dress and shoes. "Do you want something to drink," muttered Yoel. Emile raised his eyes from the drawing and lowered them again. "Do you want something to drink," Yoel asked again.

*　*　*

Many days passed.

*　*　*

Three days after she was buried they sat in the apartment. Most of the callers came in the first day. People came from the office, sat to one side, glanced out of the corner of their eyes at a folded newspaper. The Torah teacher came with his divorced wife, the principal came, followed by two pupils. "Shalom, Emile." And they handed him a black binder containing the condolences of all the children in the class on black Bristol board. With pictures passed on them. There was a drawing of the good fairy, and a drawing of the empty sky, and a drawing of a winged elevator with a little woman inside it, gliding over the sea, transparent, as if it were a glass elevator above the sun. Emile said thank you. And one of the children, whose name was Dror, and who wasn't even in the same class, took out a new tennis ball and gave it to Emile. It was me.

* * *

In the bathroom Yoel sat on the closed toilet seat with a pencil between his fingers. He moved it quickly to and fro. In the living room they asked where he was. And afterward they asked again where he was. Until in the end Emile said that he wasn't there.

* * *

And at the end of the year, at the grade one graduation ceremony, Yoel was standing to one side when the teacher signaled him to switch off the light. He asked voicelessly, "Me?" and she gestured affirmatively. And when the light went out all the children lit candles and formed a circle and began to walk, very slowly, silently, in an almost perfect circle. And Yoel waited for something to begin, the sound of an accordion, or for the teacher to strike a tambourine, or for a poem or a play or for an organ to start playing a hora or a march, but there was absolute silence in the room. The children held the candles and circled slowly. Step. Step. Pause. Step. Step. Pause.

He couldn't tell which of the flames was his. But when they started singing, he sang with all the children.

*　*　*

"People live there today, in that building. Yes, of course they do. They don't know anything, the people who live there . . . that they're living in . . . in . . . "

*　*　*

Once they went to a kind of magic show. The magician needed a volunteer from the audience.

Yoel volunteered Emile.

*　*　*

And afterward Emile went back to school. It was a fine day. They sat him where they sat him. The teacher intended to say something to the class, but she forgot. It had already been a month, after all. Perhaps it was better to let sleeping dogs lie. But the children were a little nicer to him than usual. They let him copy their work.

He didn't go on any of the annual excursions. And he received an exemption from sports as well.

Girls didn't like him.

*　*　*

And once Yoel was walking in the street. Far from home. Perhaps in Jerusalem. And suddenly he thought: Where is Emile at this exact moment? What is he doing? And he stopped. And turned round. The child was already sixteen. It didn't matter. And he directed his gaze and his heart to the west, to Tel Aviv, and pretended that he could see him, until he recovered his breath and calmed down.

* * *

After a year they went to the building together. This was the building they were supposed to live in. After the accident living there was out of the question. There was a lawyer who took care of it, they gave back the whole of the advance payment, but Yoel received no compensation for Leah. They proved that she had been negligent. That not only had there been a notice in red letters, but also nylon tape on the door. The deceased had removed the tape, ignored the warning notice, and had opened the iron door. Therefore, according to the Civil Wrongs ordinance, my client bears no personal responsibility whatsoever, either direct or indirect, for the damages of the plaintiff or the estate of the deceased.

When his lawyer came up to him looking downcast, Yoel said to him, Never mind. Without compensation's good too. It's better without compensation.

They went on living on Smuts. But after a year had passed Yoel took Emile to the building, which was now finished and occupied. Cars were parked in the street, which was empty at this early hour of the morning. They stood in front of the dark mailboxes and looked at the names of the tenants. "Here, apartment sixteen, this is where we were supposed to live." Emile ran his eyes over the names of the tenants. A voice came out of the mailbox: "Are you looking for someone?"

They stood in front of the elevator. The red numbers began to go down. 8, 7, 6. And on 1 Emile turned away and ran up the stairs, with Yoel behind him.

*   *   *

Yoel couldn't sleep. Emile lay next to him on the bed. He lay on his back. His eyes closed. He was almost ten.

The next day, when they asked him in school why he was so tired, he said that he didn't get enough sleep, because his father was turning in his grave all night long.

*   *   *

Yoel looked at the changing red numbers. The elevator was new, the old one had been taken away on the day of the accident. But the shaft was her shaft. A high grave, that was how he thought of it. He thought of saying to Emile, "This is her grave, here in the shaft," but he kept quiet, afraid of getting tangled up in his words. They went down, they didn't get out of the elevator, they waited a while and went up again. Then they went down again, up, down, as Emile would do on his own dozens of times after that, in the same building and in other buildings. Yoel switched on the fan but it was hot as an oven in there. And after a few minutes people knocked angrily on the door with the keys to their mailboxes. Yoel and Emile didn't notice the knocks. They went up and down, the doors didn't open, 1, 2, 3, 4, 5, 6, 7, and back again. They surrendered to the repetitive rhythm. More people arrived, new keys banging on the steel door. Until they gave up and called the elevator maintenance company, a technician arrived, stopped the elevator, and brought it up to the next floor under manual control. It's gone haywire, he thought, but when the doors opened he saw them, first reflected in the big mirror and then in the flesh, standing huddled together, their profiles to the mirror and to him. The boy trembling, the man in a yellow plastic helmet, with a little trickle of blood coming out of his nose.

*　*　*

Or, for example, they were walking down the street and Emile suddenly began to run. He saw her at the end of the road. And afterward the two of them would walk back up the street holding cups of water somebody had given them. The water wobbled in the two cups. One high one low. Emile looked at his father. At how he held the cup of water. At how he walked. And he tried to copy the way he walked. How he held. How he raised the plastic cup to his lips. And Yoel never even noticed that he was being imitated.

*　*　*

There was a candle burning there. And somebody held out to it the wick of another candle that had gone out. And wonder of wonders it caught fire immediately. In spite of the wet. In spite of the fact that it was already black. In spite of the fact that it had gotten very short. But nobody noticed. They didn't pay any attention to it. They clapped their hands, sang Happy Birthday. And somebody brought out an accordion. The children wrote greetings in the letters they had just learned.

*   *   *

Once Yoel dreamed that he was looking at his digital watch, and the time was 5:17, and then it changed straight to 5:19, and all day after that he was nervous and depressed because of the dream. And he dreamed too that he was trying on a shirt with buttons, and the shirt was too small, to his surprise. And he also dreamed that someone was leading him out of an apartment in London, and Buckingham Palace and the National Gallery were standing there in the backyard, and he was overjoyed, even though he could see that the palace walls were full of repairs, like swollen veins visible through the skin. And he turned over in bed in his dream and his hand touched Emile's shoulder, who was dreaming that he had gone on a class trip to Jerusalem, and the leader of the trip was an army officer, and he, Emile, wants to go home in the middle of the trip and he's sure that if they would only let him go he'd be able to get back to Tel Aviv on his own, and in the bus he sees the mother of one of his classmates, and he asks her permission to go back alone, and she says, there's no need to go alone, I'm going back in any case, let's slip away without the soldier noticing, and he sees the officer reading a newspaper, and they leave quietly through the back door of the bus, and he thinks that it's strange that she's taking **him** home but leaving her son behind. And he muttered something in his sleep, the room was dark but there was a dim light flickering in the passage, and Yoel heard the muttering and pulled the blanket over him in his sleep, and Buckingham Palace turned into a cathedral in Milan, which he had once visited with Leah, "Before you were born," and someone told him to come and see what was **behind** the cathedral, and he said to Leah, I'll be back in a minute, I'm just going with this gentleman, and the gentleman led him by the hand along the great cathedral wall and then inside the wall, the wall turned out to be hollow, gradually the crowd of tourists dwindled, gradually it grew dark, and it seemed that they would never arrive at their destination, and Yoel asked him, in the dream it was Italian, When will the wall end? Only then he became aware that they were riding through the wall in a kind of little coach, and the signor took a sharp right, and there was the torn, red tape, and someone told him that they had found the bones of a lion here in Italy, what do you say to that. And Emile, in his sleep, heard Yoel's sharp cry on seeing the lion. And he was a puppet. He was wrapped in coarse salt. And he flew through the clouds. In the morning his father explained to him, "It's because of the play you saw last week in Jerusalem." He dreamed that he was slowly turning into a wooden child, and that his father was pulling his strings, but he didn't tell Yoel this. "And what did you say in your dream," Yoel asked him, spreading blackberry jam on a slice of bread and handing it to him, and Emile thought for a minute and suddenly said, "Daddy, pick me up," and Yoel said "What?" in a weak, surprised voice, and Emile said that now he remembered, his strings had snapped.

הרבה מזל טוב ושמח"ת וחיים שלמים

[Many congratulations and may you live a full life]

[   ]–EMILE

In days to come she would remember a blinding light and the noise of an engine. This was the passage. In a ship? A bus? As if the Mediterranean were a single neighborhood, and her family had moved from Cairo Street to Jaffa Street. To the city of Jaffa, that is.

When President Sadat of Egypt came to enjoy the intoxicating air of *Eretz Yisrael*—in other words, to take some of it back—the Israeli Prime Minister's bureau organized a deputation of children. The children of Egypt, that is. The idea being that they would go to the President and tell him how happy they were in their new country. They thought, he would hear a little Egyptian Arabic, sentimental tears would moisten his eyes, and he would concede a few square meters. From Begin's bureau the emissaries set out on their urgent mission, Egyptian Jews were collected from all over Israel. The project was widely covered in the press. Some of these emissaries had never even heard of Anwar Sadat, they thought that Nasser was the king. Some were afraid to go, because who knows, perhaps they would force them to stay, or harm their relatives who had stayed behind.

The bureau reached the home of [   ] and [   ] as well. They knocked on the door. The couple was not yet living in the apartment opposite the central bus station, but a little farther south, between Jaffa and Tel Aviv, on a street that didn't have a name, just a number. The representatives arrived, they knocked on the door. Good afternoon Mrs. [   ], they said in Egyptian Arabic in order to check her accent (that's all we need, right, Ashkenazi Jews speaking university Arabic to the President), and she passed the test but she didn't want to go. She didn't want to meet President Sadat. What have I to do with him, she asked. I've forgotten Cairo. I didn't leave anything there. I came here when I was only a few days old. I don't remember anything from there! They said to her, Mrs. [   ], you don't understand, the meeting is very important, after the Jewish delegation the President will go to meet with the Prime Minister, and that's when the agreement will be finalized, so much will depend on the President's mood, and we're begging you. They had received instructions to enlist them all, especially the women, particularly the pretty women.

She was then nearly thirty. And she was very pretty indeed. They already had three men, but not a single woman. And of course, it was important for there to be a woman. They hinted at favors, at special housing. Levinsky Street, we have a vacant apartment . . . a new building, a quiet neighborhood . . . they said to her, you're still young, one day you'll have a child, think about higher education, savings . . . but she didn't want to hear.

The next day Begin arrived at the apartment to speak to her in person.

As was his habit, he traveled by bus in order not to attract attention. As in the days of the underground, he dressed simply. That green sweater. He hadn't shaved. He stopped on the way to eat a sandwich. Nobody recognized him. In his sunglasses, his clumsy muffler, his crumpled hat.

He knocked at the door. [   ] was lying in bed, the newspaper spread out next to her. He came in. She looked at him and said, "Shalom . . . Mr. Begin, Prime Minister . . . "

He waved his hand dismissively, as if it wasn't important.

They went to sit in the living room. He looked around. Empty walls. A pot plant. Two rooms. A musical instrument leaning against the couch. A kind of guitar.

"I wanted to ask . . . the boys were here yesterday . . . "

"I had no idea it was so important."

"We wanted to organize an attractive deputation."

"But me . . . of all people . . . "

"The boys investigated a lot of possibilities . . . they thought that you, Madam . . . so young . . . "

"And what would I say to him? What would we talk about?"

"Perhaps you could tell him how wonderful Cairo is in your memory, in winter, when the rain washes the bazaars."

"But my memories of it are so small . . . Mainly I remember my mother's face, to tell the truth."

"And yet, happy memories of the capital city, a short description of the streets crowded with people . . . "

"But all I remember are pictures, three pictures . . . "

"Three pictures, wonderful, wonderful, more than enough, a short conversation . . . "

"Well, for the sake of peace . . . "

"For the sake of peace, precisely, yes, that's what I'm saying, for the sake of peace."

"The rain? The bazaars?"

"Luxor . . . Alexandria . . . the Nile . . . "

"But I never went to . . . "

"In any case, in any case, perhaps you could devote a little of your time to research, write down a few things, in praise of the land of your birth, yes . . . "

"More tea? Perhaps a slice of cake?"

I won't say no, I won't say no, ah, a small slice . . . I won't say no."

And the week after that they came to fetch her. [   ] switched on the television as soon as she left and sat up close. The convoy drove to Jerusalem with another three Egyptians, two from Haifa and one from Be'er Sheba. One of the Egyptians opened his mouth and said, "This was the hardest week of my life," and the man from Be'er Sheba said, "I haven't slept for two nights." And the three of them looked at [   ], who said, "I was actually born here, more or less."

They asked her where her parents were from and of course it turned out that they all knew each other. And they were quite excited in anticipation of their meeting with the Egyptian President, which was canceled in the end due to scheduling changes. And the four of them hung around for an hour or two waiting for someone to approach them. To take them back home at least. But who had the time to worry about them, when the agreement was about to be signed. They sat to one side in the entrance hall of the Knesset building. The older man from Haifa asked her, this time in Arabic, if she was married. She said that she was, and he said, "That's a pity, we have a son, he'll be thirty at Chanukkah, never married, a real he-man," and he fell silent. She wanted to tell him that she had gotten pregnant and that she had a son, and that her son should be nine years old now, in the third grade, and that she sometimes thought of becoming a teacher, and going up every year to "his class," and perhaps, even if he wasn't in her school, perhaps they would come to play on the football field in the afternoon, she thought, children from that other school, and she would recognize him. But of course she had never finished so much as ten years of school herself and how could she be a teacher. At the age of sixteen she got pregnant and her whole life changed. She left school, went to learn sewing. And then she was swallowed up in the textile plant.

And the younger man from Haifa asked her, "How do we get out of here," and she said, "They'll come to get us," and someone walked past in a safari suit, as if he was going to hunt elephants, and she said to the elephant hunter that he should go to Begin and tell him that they had been left there, and the man in the safari suit looked at her for a minute as if the bench they were sitting on had suddenly spoken to him, then he walked away without giving her a second glance. And half an hour later they got up and went to look for a bus to take them to the central bus station and send them on their separate ways, the young and old men from Haifa to Haifa, [   ] to Tel Aviv, and the man from Be'er Sheba to Netanya, once he was already out of Be'er Sheba he might as well take a bit of a holiday on the beach, and there he would meet a tourist from France, and after a few months they would get married and he would go with her to Arles, and they would live there for many years, and one day, when he already had French citizenship and four sons whose names would almost certainly be Abraham and Isaac and Jacob and François, they would take a trip together to Egypt and walk down the street where he was born, and someone would recognize him.

And when they stopped at the central bus station in Jerusalem and parted to take their various buses, a bus arrived full of schoolchildren who had been brought there to wave Egyptian flags in honor of the President on his way from the Knesset to the Holocaust memorial museum, and among them was Emile. That's the whole story. They were very close to each other there in the station, maybe thirty meters. But there were a lot of other children there too.

סיפור

היה היה בית בת גו
אורי. ואורי היו גרבים
שבבות.

[A Story. Once there was a house. In the house lived Uri. Uri had naughty socks.]

How many years did they have together? Six minus two months.

At the age of five and something Emile wrote a story. And they didn't even know that he knew how to write. That is, he wrote an occasional letter, maybe a short word or two. And one day he brought his mother the page. **A story. Once there was a house.**

In the house lived Uri. Uri had naughty socks. Next to the story he had drawn a kind of curly shape with a purple marker. Maybe the socks, she thought. Leah stood holding the page in her hand. She read the words again and again. A sentence in Hebrew. And another one. And another one. Emile saw her eyes running to and fro. She asked: "Who's Uri," and Emile thought for a minute and said, "I don't know." And then he said, as if surprised by the question, "The child in the story," and he added: "There's no such child."

Leah said, describe the house to me. And he said, it's just like here. Leah said, and Uri? And he said, just like me. And she said, "Once, when?" And he said, today, tomorrow. And she said, what are naughty socks? And he laughed.

Leah put the story between two little plates of glass and hung it in their room. And Yoel, who came home from work in the evening and took off his shoes, went into the bedroom to "lie down for a bit and read something," and as he was arranging his neck in a comfortable position and folding his thin pillow with one hand while holding volume one of *Joseph and his Brothers* in the other, he saw the story on the wall. Strange, he thought, that wasn't there before. He didn't understand what he was seeing. As if he didn't know the language. He left Joseph and his brothers and got closer to the picture. "Leah," he called from the room, not noticing that she was standing there. "Leah," he called out. "What," she whispered from the half-open door. "Who's Uri," asked Yoel, a slight panic rising in his voice. Leah burst out laughing. Yoel threw himself back onto the bed.

* * *

From the next room Emile heard their laughter and he laughed too.

* * *

And one day, a few hours after Emile came home from school, the teacher called up in excitement and said, how wonderful, how thrilling, what a miracle, her husband of course was from a religious family, an act of Providence. And Yoel, who had fallen asleep in his armchair, finding volume one of *Joseph and his Brothers* difficult, yawned into the receiver and said, yes, of course, but what exactly are you talking about? And who exactly are you, if I may ask? And she said, "What am I talking about? What kind of a question is that? About the fact that your wife isn't actually dead after all." And a bayonet jabbed at Yoel's heart and he said, she isn't, oh. And the teacher heard the tone of his voice and hesitated. And it came out that Emile was telling stories at school. In other words, making things up.

The boy had told them that she was in the hospital and the doctors said that she had seemed dead because she was really **like** dead, but suddenly she held out her hand and asked for a glass of water, and Emile just happened to be there at that exact minute, holding a glass of cold water in his hand, and he gave it to her to drink. And he told them that she was a piano teacher, and that she said to her students, "Now is when it has to hurt." Where did he get that from? He told them that she played with an orchestra in Scotland, and that his father was the conductor of the orchestra

124

("What, that's not true either?")

And Emile told a lot of other stories too. The teacher only heard some of them. Some the children heard. But most of them were only heard by the two walls of Emile's corner in the schoolyard, and by the sand trapped inside the angle of that corner whose vertex was here and whose suburbs were out in infinity. There was the story about the stockings that rescued his mother from the elevator, pulled her up so that she was in midair when the elevator hit the ground. Or when he said that she was a driving instructor. So sometimes she had to travel far away. In order to teach them how to drive up steep rises. In Jerusalem. In Haifa. Or she was a cook in a restaurant at the North Pole. He never told the story about the naughty socks again. He forgot it. But Yoel didn't forget. He lay on his back for an hour or two. A meeting had been canceled. Suddenly a couple of hours were yawning ahead of him. He removed the socks from his sandaled feet. It was half autumn half spring. And a pleasant breeze came to caress his toes. And his socks lay stinking inside out on the lawn in front of him. Shade danced on the treetops and the ground. It danced on the arms of Yoel Zisu. He put his sandals on his socks, and remembered Emile's story, which now hung next to the angel. How did it go? "There was a child . . . the child lived in a house . . . the child had socks . . . the child's name was . . . Emile had naughty socks . . . " He cocked his head and looked at his socks. A hole in one heel. Empty and inside out they lay there, mostly beneath his left-foot sandal. And when he turned his head to the right, to the other side of the lawn, Leah was there. Unexpectedly, she wasn't crushed. Nor was she covered with blood. But Yoel knew that inside all her organs were smashed. From the force of the blow. Eight floors. A thousand times he had imagined the blow. Had she been smashed into the ceiling. Sometimes you lose consciousness on the way down, the doctor said, trying to comfort him, from the fright. The heart goes into arrest, it stops beating. Yoel stretched out his right hand and placed it in her hand. It was the same hand that he remembered. The fingers were Leah's slender fingers. How could he mistake them? Not that his hand was very big. But hers was smaller. You could see it was a woman's hand. The fingernails she would alternately bite and manicure. Now they were bitten. The sorrow would not pass, he knew. But in order not to make things difficult for her he said, yes, it's passing. I've taken up my life again. She tightened her fingers a little on his. What a terrible mistake you made, he said to her. Getting into an elevator before the engineer's inspection. If only I'd come with you. And he wanted to tell her that he forgave her for the mistake, but he couldn't pronounce the words. If only I'd come. Perhaps she didn't press "stop." Perhaps she pressed the bell instead of the stop button. Listen, he said to her, a mistake like that, who makes a mistake like that . . . You were always so responsible about everything. You balanced our checkbook. You switched the gas off two times over. And turned off all the lights. Read the small print on boxes of food. You paid our bills two weeks in advance. So as not to leave it till the last minute. You went to the post office, kept the receipts in a file. So how, how, how. Getting into the elevator in an unfinished building. You, who would water the flowers every Sunday, Tuesday, and Thursday. How could you do it. How did you not take care. When you had a six-year-old child.

Yoel's fingers gripped his socks. The birds sang as if day was breaking. Leah didn't answer.

THE CITY

And the head of the city is raised to the blue sky, and a great shadow falls over the whole city, over the whole continent, as in an eclipse, and they see, in the last minutes of their lives, a sight that is both terrible and beautiful, an alien visitor, not **from** another planet, for the planet itself is the visitor, a comet, or an asteroid, tearing through the atmosphere and boiling the seas dry, racing like a locomotive without a driver, millions look at it and millions more look at their television screens, and one thought is multiplied by a billion, a dream, it's only a dream, and we will surely wake up from it. And it's impossible to look anywhere but at the sky, where they can already see, at its farthest edges, where they know, where they can see. And at night a kind of whistling seems to come from the clouds. Everyone has known for months that it's going to happen, the calculations were flawless, they know the exact hour, and where it will hit, the scientists gave the longitude, the latitude, artists built giant sculptures at the predicted points of collision and set up cameras, and high-school students put the data into equations and prayed for a miracle, but all the calculations showed a single result, nobody was mistaken. They knew the name of the city, and the inhabitants of the city were supposed to leave, but they stayed. Some of them because they weren't completely convinced by these scientific predictions—but most of them just to see.

[   ]

A child crosses the road and goes into the apartment opposite and disappears, and his life is no longer the same. At the beginning, he thought, the child would be different from his adoptive parents. He isn't used to them. But then, like a cut, the wound heals. After a few months, maybe after a few days. And then the parents change and the child changes until they meet at a point in the middle. Like three stars. No: two planets and a moon, he thought. He raised his head to the sky. In the end the system stabilizes, gravity lays down the law. The moon revolves around them and they revolve around each other. And the real father, the birth father, burns far away and warms them. Like the sun. From very far away. And the years pass. And over the course of the years, from a statistical point of view, he thinks, if the child and the parents who gave him up live in the same city (he had no way of knowing, of course, but he felt, very strongly, that this was the case), they must pass each other every few years. And there's a chance that they even ride the same bus. Even on the same seats. There's even a chance—a small chance—that the child gets up to give his seat to one of his parents without knowing who they are. And someone on the bus sees that they resemble each other, in other words, precisely, the stranger understands that they are father and son. Is there anything more natural than a father and son taking the bus together? And therefore nobody says anything, nobody stands up and makes a fuss. And they ride another stop or two and get off the bus. Or, at a concert, they sit two rows apart. Or on the beach. Or they pass each other in two elevators in an office building, one going up, one going down, between them only a thin partition. And the movement.

Like a man running over a dog at night, and nobody sees and nobody blames him, but the dog won't give him any peace. And he sees dogs in the street, and the next day he starts taking out a little water to give to the dogs. There aren't any stray dogs anymore, the thought suddenly strikes him. They've exterminated them all. Only cats left. Or like a man who has been robbed of his hand, and the robber is walking close by, still holding on to his hand. You could say that this is how he feels.

Drifting slowly in the green current, a sail without a ship, the swollen plastic bag makes its way east. Dipping slightly in the water, most of it in the air. From a statistical point of view, thought [   ]. From a statistical point of view. And he looked away, turning his back to the river. From a statistical point of view it may be that at exactly that moment Emile and his two adoptive parents were gliding past in a wooden boat. And Yoel was rowing. And

Leah was shading her eyes against the sun with her hand. And Emile was sleeping at the bottom of the boat, his head on a coiled rope. And by the time [   ] looked back again, the boat had already disappeared round the bend in the river.

It didn't happen like that.

He looked back again. The plastic bag was no longer there. But if he had only remained there a little longer, five months and two days and three minutes, his thought would have coincided with the sight of that boat passing there. In reality.

Luckily for him, he didn't know this.

[   ]

She also had a cat.

For nights she couldn't sleep. She loved it. What? What was its name? The cat's name was Max and Moritz. It had two names.

Every day it climbed onto the bed and went to sleep. It did this all the time. But one day, in winter, it fell asleep on top of the blanket. And she stood facing the blanket, what to do, if she pulled the blanket the cat would wake up. On the other hand, it was cold . . . in the end she lay down carefully next to Max and Moritz, and fell asleep. Covered herself, so to speak, with the pillow. [   ], her husband, was away at the time. Traveling. It was the end of the tax year and he was a bookkeeper. The oud remained at home, in its case. And the cat smacked it, over and over again.

In the morning she woke up stiff and chilly. The cat looked at her as if it was expecting something. Which it was.

She went down to the store and bought it a chicken. She jointed the chicken, cut off pieces of flesh, pounded them, for the cat to eat. Eat up. She served it. She roasted livers, necks. And Max and

Moritz came. It smelled the chicken, came to the room to eat. If she took too long at the butcher's, it got very angry. If she was a little late with the chicken it made a scene. Once it even scratched her. And if she shut it in the room, for instance, say she wanted to read, it would open the door. It knew how.

Sometimes she thought that the cat was the devil. The devil incarnate. So fat, half a chicken every day, and it liked hot milk too . . . maybe she should strangle it . . . throw it in the fire . . .

But that same day it climbed onto her bed again. And once she dreamed that it was raping her. It wasn't exactly a cat, or exactly a man, a kind of half-cat half-man, and it dug its claws into her and raped her, hard. She whimpered, no, no, but nothing helped. From then on it would rape her from time to time. She almost got used to it.

There was one thing she feared above all. This was the fear that they would bring her a social worker. A social worker, yes. A social worker.

Bring for what? Bring who, exactly? Never mind. Please just leave me alone.

Now her throat was sore. The cat climbed onto the blanket again. The whole blanket was already full of cat hairs. Her handbag was covered with them too. They didn't come off with water. They stuck there, as if they were growing right out of the leather of the bag, like hairs growing out of a body.

How her husband hated the cat. And her mother, how frightened she was of it. When her mother would come to visit, [   ] would shut Max and Moritz in the bedroom. Not that her mother came to visit. Not ever. She only phoned to check if [   ] was

133

still alive. And hung up immediately.

[   ] locked all the doors because she was afraid they would send a social worker.

But the cat would open them.

And it knew how to answer the phone as well.

EMILE

And once he watched a horror movie on television. All he remembered later on was someone saying the words "try to remember" over and over again. There was something about hypnosis, a pendulum clock, red cards, and a man with white skin and a scar sewn into his cheek, and he looked straight at the camera (but Emile didn't know there was a camera there), and his eyes suddenly began to drip black ink.

Yoel, who watched the last few seconds in horrified indignation from the corner of the living room, crossed the room with a doughnut in his hand, and covered Emile's eyes, stretching out his leg and trying to turn off the television with his foot. The television fell with a crash and Leah came into the room. From today on there won't be anymore of this garbage here. Finished. She was getting rid of the television for good. And Emile, with the movie ruined right at the good bit, was furious and he started to yell that if she got rid of the television he would run away from home. And she said, "Go ahead, run away, nobody's keeping you here by force." And all at once he escalated things: "I want you to give me back, I want to go back, take another child, take the sick one instead of me, take the **uncle**."

He liked horror movies from an early age. He never grew out of it. There was a book he read, where they buried someone alive while he was sleeping. They put him to sleep, moved him to the yard next door, to a pit they had prepared for him in advance. And when he woke up he was already buried inside it. Emile read the book again and again. And then it got into his dreams.

Yoel sat down in the living room, but kept quiet throughout the quarrel. The yelling grew louder. Emile tried to turn on the television, which was lying on its back like a poisoned cockroach, Leah disconnected it. Emile started to shriek in a deafening soprano. The neighbors' light went on. Yoel kept quiet. Pretended to read a book. He even turned the page and moved his finger. Leah looked in his direction and screamed, Why don't you do something. Yoel didn't raise his head. She screamed at him again, some stinging insult or other. You and your books. Then he said, without raising his eyes from the book, "Okay, go and get dressed. Let's go." Emile stopped screaming at once. Yoel spoke again, in a matter-of-fact tone, "Put on your sandals, Emile, let's go," and he stood up, with his finger in the book.

I remember his finger, I began to tremble, I'll never forget that trembling, that overwhelming fear, like a truck racing in my direction, like a plane losing altitutde, like burning sand sucking you in, I'll never forget it, never, and I looked at him, to double check, see if he was joking, but he said, "Come on, put on your sandals, they'll be closing up there soon. Do you want to be left without a bed to sleep in tonight? Do you want to have to sleep in the same bed as the uncle?" And he stood next to the front door and turned the key noisily, and I walked toward the door sweating and trembling, and I'll never forget him standing next to the door with the keys, and I'll never forget him whistling, and I walked toward the door hanging my head, and my mother, I think it was no more than two or three months before the accident, stood at the other end of the room and said, "Yoel . . ." but that was all.

I sank into a black abyss. I wish I could just say "I fainted." In my dreams, years later, I would go into that white house, with all those disgusting children, and there was one child there who was actually a big, brown cockroach, with long feelers, which they said was why his parents had left him there. Who would want to have a child like that? And I was always there on my own, he didn't even want to go inside with me and accompany me to my old crib. He put me down in the snow at the door and drove away immediately, before I even had time to look back.

THE CITY

A path of wet sand and gravel. For days the rain has been beating down on it. What was once a proper path has turned into a stagnant river of mud. Hailstones hit the stones on the ground. Solitary trees on the far horizon. Gray. And electricity poles. Torn cables. The rain comes down, strong and slanting. From time to time thunder or lightning. Open fields in the distance. Grayness in all directions. And mist. Sunlight doesn't penetrate, it's blocked. The clouds hang low, covering the sky in layers. Open fields from horizon to horizon. And everything's empty, completely empty. And only the rain comes down. Where is everybody? Where are they hiding? Hullo! Hullo! Is there anybody in those houses? Hullo! Hullo! Is there anybody who knows what happened? Hullo! Hullo! Hullo! Where are we, what is this place? Hullo! Hullo! Can you hear? Can you hear me at all?

YOEL–EMILE

Yoel woke up and went on lying in bed a little longer. What's that noise, like a rat gnawing in the closet? It's early, still early, he thought, it's still early. One day in the winter of '88 Emile got up in the morning and started packing a bag, and Yoel, who woke up a little after him because of the noise coming from what was once Leah's study and had turned in the course of time into a storeroom, went to the room and asked him, Emile, what's going on, it's five in the morning, and Emile, without looking up from the bag, said, "It's the day," and Yoel asked again, what, what day, did I forget something? And Emile looked up to see if Yoel was pretending or joking, but no, he was serious, he really didn't remember, and Emile didn't know how to react, but he took a breath and said into the bag, Dad, the draft. Today's the draft. Only yesterday I told you it was tomorrow, and before that, twenty times, why are you pretending to be so astonished. And Emile was embarrassed by his own anger and laughed a little, but his laughter annoyed Yoel. "What's there to laugh about?" And Yoel said no, no-no, you said "It's tomorrow" and I thought

139

you were talking about, I don't know, a soccer game, I was too lazy to ask, you said "It's tomorrow," I didn't understand, I wasn't concentrating. When, asked Yoel, when is it happening did you say? And Emile sat on the floor and put his hands on his head. "Today," he said almost whispering. "When?" asked his father, as if he hadn't heard. "When? Tomorrow—?"

And two hours later Yoel was sitting in the kitchen, the keys still in his pocket, after taking Emile to the induction center, and he didn't know if he was supposed to get out and accompany him, how long would he be allowed to accompany him, until he put on his uniform, until the shots, surely they gave them shots, maybe they'd say, "Hold him so he doesn't squirm, Daddy," like they'd said when Emile was small. And perhaps until he received his rank, presumably they sewed on the rank and issued them with weapons, and perhaps today they allowed the parents to accompany them even further, perhaps right up to the gates of the boot camp, he thought, but when Emile got out of the car Yoel didn't switch off the engine, and he waved good-bye to him from his seat, and Emile looked at him for a minute, and when he understood that he was on his own he said, "Okay then, good-bye for now," and Yoel said, "Get in touch when you can," and Emile said, "Are you going straight home from here?" And Yoel replied, "Maybe I'll stop somewhere for breakfast, I know there's—" but the cars behind them were already blowing their horns, recruits impatient to begin their induction, not to miss the racing train of mobilization, and he turned away and drove off, and stopped the windshield wipers, and when he looked for Emile in the mirror there were only a few girl soldiers there.

And Yoel drove home and suddenly he was home, and he went up and made himself a cup of tea but for some reason the water didn't boil, and the teabag lay in the lukewarm water, and he took a sip and spat it out. And he opened the door of the fridge on his leg, and dropped ice cubes by mistake on his toes, and afterward he drank boiling-hot tea and burned his tongue, and he spat on the back of his hand and burned his hand too, and when he raised his head he hit it on the corner of the kitchen cupboard.

The sergeant barber looked at Emile and asked him, "So how do you like it? Short?" and Emile said, "Leave me what you can," and the barber sniggered and said, "I'm joking, you idiot. Here the clipper is always on the shortest setting," and he kissed his clipper. And another barber, busy demolishing the dreadlocks of someone sitting deflated and dejected next to Emile, said in an ingratiating voice, "Don't ask me where your hair's going to. Don't ask. You don't want to know. The army just adores your hair, darlings," and he banged his huge clippers on the table to clear as blockage. They're like what they use for shearing sheep, thought Emile. Snip, snip.

And Yoel, in the kitchen, said, there's still a chance, maybe it won't happen, maybe it's just pre, pre-enlistment, pre-draft, maybe they'll send him to a class, he'll probably be back today, it's probably just verification, immunization, physical examinations . . . and he looked at Emile's picture next to Leah's on the kitchen wall. Born 1970, uniform and weapon 1988. Who is he anyway, he said in a whisper, how can he suddenly be eighteen years old? Where were we yesterday? What happened yesterday? He couldn't remember anything. And last week? A stab of pain pierced the side of his stomach. He noticed that his tea was cold. "Why do they keep recruiting them all the time?" he said suddenly to the stove.

The barber shut the big bin and sat on it. And Yoel suddenly stood up. And he started walking quickly round the house. Emile looked at his watch. It was ten in the morning. The heating was on high. How long was it going to take? Half an hour, an hour. "The chain of induction," they told them. In the meantime stand here. There was apparently a problem with the kitbags. They told them they were waiting for kitbags, but the storeroom was locked. The store-man was on sick leave. Wait here in the meantime. The clipped hairs on his neck were scratching him and he tried to shake them off. But the barber had sprayed him with something and the hairs stuck to his skin like leeches. Someone tried to sit down, but immediately there was a shout, "No sitting, what do you think you're doing, up on your feet." Yoel must be sitting in one of the Or Yehuda kebab joints now and eating charcoal grilled meat, Emile thought. At home vegetables, outside barbeque. At home raw kohlrabi, outside skewered livers. He sensed, he couldn't yet completely understand it, that the draft had torn him from his father irreversibly, and even if he went home today or tomorrow or at the end of the week—suddenly he realized that he didn't know where he would stay tonight, where he would sleep, for the first time in his life—the way he had left home today had made a tear in his life which would never be mended, and his father, who had preferred in recent months to ignore Emile's approaching mobilization and to bury his head in the sand and pretend to be astonished at his induction, which Yoel had almost missed, which he'd almost slept through as Emile left the house, his father was solely to blame for his situation, for his standing here in this stinking room—one of the inductees had farted and another had responded in kind, and voices were raised in laughter on his left—and it was clear to him, to Emile, that if Yoel was standing next to him now he would be capable of strangling him to death. And then he took fright at this thought, like a person discovering a mouse in his house and recoiling, stepping breathlessly backward. He was unable to get rid of his hatred immediately. All of a sudden the mouse would be there again. Skipping and scampering and darting at him. Yoel looked around him as if someone was tapping on the windows. "Wait wait, tomorrow you'll get weapons," said someone, "tomorrow you'll start to sweat." And Emile felt how his shorn hair was only the first step on the way to a deeper cut that the army was going to make in his soul, how the scissors would enter into his mind and soul and cut and cut. And Yoel said to himself that there was no doubt he would shoot someone, he would shoot an Arab, and nothing would happen to him, they wouldn't even arrest him, they would let him off him with a wink, and Emile suddenly winked, twice, and Yoel knew that Emile would also use a club, he would beat someone, and a bone snapped in Yoel's mind.

And all of a sudden he wanted to shout for someone to get him out of there, for his father to come in now, right now, and make his way in the heat through the crowd of exhausted recruits and present his adoption papers and Leah's death certificate (which he had once seen folded up in his father's drawer under the bedside radio), and explain that there had been a mistake, and that they had no right to take him at all, as an only son and an only adopted son what's more, and they would bow their heads and admit their mistake, and he would go home in the rain, he would take no notice of the pouring rain, all he wanted was to get home, at home they'll take care of you, free of worries you'll lie in bed at home, someone will know what to put on your bread and someone will know how much sugar to put in your tea, and Mommy will be waiting for you at home, and when she sees your uniform she'll burst out laughing. And he'll take off the uniform and throw it out the window, and as on a suddenly canceled school day the three of them will go to the sea, and already a crisp cold watermelon is cut open for them, this is your lucky day, the last one left over from the summer, and someone suddenly smacked him on the back of his neck and said, "Hey shellshock, what's your problem? Yallah, move it," and Emile, still feeling the blow on the back of his neck, turned sideways allowing one of the soldiers from the medical corps holding a plastic basket full of rattling syringes to pass.

Somewhere in the room someone burst into tears. I can't, I can't, he wept, I'm not cut out for it, I want to leave, I didn't want to come. I didn't say anything about my knee problem, it hurts me in winter, look, it's starting already, I want a medical review, I was raised wrapped up in cottonwool, I can't go on, I've had it, I'm finished. "What a bummer," said somebody else, and it wasn't clear if he was referring to the recruit's knees or to the situation as a whole. What a bummer, what a bummer. The time was 10:39 in the morning on the first day of the army. Through the window Emile heard somebody say, "The chain's stuck again, they're not

144

letting any more in," and somebody else said, "So why not let them out on the other end, to relieve the pressure," and the first one replied, "Impossible, they've already started the induction process, what, are you going stick their hair back on? The little shits have already received their serial numbers, what can we do?" The crying soldier wouldn't calm down. He said to someone, apparently his friend, who from time to time looked round and smiled at all the rest as if to reassure them, "I'm not cut out for things like this. I've never left home before, I want to sleep in my own bed, I'm dying, I'm dying, I'm not built for this, I haven't got any cartilage in my right knee, I hid my knee problems, when it rains it hurts me something awful, I've been wrapped in cottonwool from day one, I never went out into the world." And someone said to Emile, "He's dying already? Wait till they start hazing us, wait till they start with guard duty half the night, wait till they start with Saturdays confined to base. Not built for it? Don't worry, they'll build him, that's what we came for, cartilage, they'll give him cartilage made of rubber, the sonofabitch, cottonwool he wants? Steel wool is what he'll get, tank wool, the maniac."

Far away in a kitchen in Tel Aviv, Yoel stared into Leah's eyes and she looked back at him over the pots and pans standing on the stove. And he washed his face in the kitchen sink and dried his eyes with the greasy kitchen towel. And advanced, threateningly, on the picture, his face twisted like that of an enraged thug. And stood close up. And suddenly turned back and saw the neighbor from next door standing and looking at him behind the blinds.

[   ]

And a few months before Emile was drafted, in the summer of
'88, [   ] saw an article in the paper about that year's draft, and
she said to her husband, he's eighteen, we celebrated his birthday
at Passover, he must be going into the army now. I can see him in
a uniform. I'm telling you, this summer he's going into the army,
they take everybody in the summer. And I'm telling you, they'll
see a brown child and they'll put him in a combat unit. They'll
take him for the tanks, for guarding the border. They'll give him
a gun. We have to do something. We have to get him out of the
army.

He husband looked at her, his jaw dropping. He stopped playing.
The oud made a dull noise when he put it down on the floor.

And over the next three years she read the newspaper to see the
names of the wounded and the dead, to see their pictures. One
day, she knew, she would see his picture and she would recognize

him at once, even if his name was . . . she was unable to invent another name. Every name would be a bad name.

Three years. She would check the birthdates of all the fallen and the wounded. And if there were days with no reports of casualties, they were days of great relief. She made a list. Three years. And then another year. In case his draft had been deferred.

And after a year she saw a picture, after some "important operation," and she said (as she'd said several times before and after that): it's him. For sure. He looks like [   ]. Just like him. She checked the time of the funeral. Suddenly everything became clear. In the paper it said, born in 1970. Her heart fell between her lungs, burned the inside of her body. She thought they would write "adopted," but they didn't write anything. Not in the other papers either. Of course not, of course, the child was dead, why should they say adopted. It was him. It was him. She read his new name. She couldn't remember it. She didn't tell her husband. He didn't want to hear about it. He refused to acknowledge the possibility at all. He immersed himself more and more in his leisurely improvisations.

"The army? What army?"

With little nail scissors she cut out the death notice. The next day she was the first one in the military cemetery. She sat under the tree next to the big water faucet.

The coffin appeared. The members of the family, bathed in tears, flushed, in black clothes. Soldiers wearing dark glasses. Skullcaps creased in quarters.

The lips of the faucet were wet. Salivating.

She mingled with the family, dressed in black like them, her tears absorbed in theirs. Supported on either side by grieving aunts. Nobody knew her. Nobody asked.

Once she found herself sitting in a café, in Haifa, on the pavement. There were two glass ashtrays on the table in front of her, full of gray water and cigarette stubs. She didn't understand what was happening to her. Until somebody walked past and drew her attention to the fact that she was sitting in the rain.

They fired the customary shots in the air. The commanding officer delivered the eulogy.

After the ceremony she followed the mourners to their private bus. Two soldiers stood at the doorway. She bowed her head, climbed the steps. Soldiers with loaded guns were sitting there. She wanted to ask them. But to ask them what, exactly.

They arrived at a dark apartment. The television set was turned upside down. Unwashed fruit stood on the table. Carpets stood, rolled up, in the four corners of the living room. The boy's picture had been enlarged. With a black ribbon across it. And hung up. Was it him. Maybe. Definitely not. Maybe. Beyond a doubt . . . no. Almost twenty years had passed. She couldn't allow herself to be absolutely sure. She clung to the vestiges of hope. But her toes were already dipped in that lake, in the heart of the distant, impassable forest, down narrow steps, with the smell of mold, and the smell of fire. Heavier and heavier. With every step. And it was hard to breathe. Looking for a place to lean. And there was no place.

She sat down among the relatives. She declined the cookies.

Peeked from time to time. After a while the father entered. Holding the son's black beret in both hands. He crushed the beret, he squeezed it, he wiped his weeping face with it. He looked round. Nobody went up to him. "Where's Giora," he suddenly shouted, "where is he, the bastard, where are you, where's Giora, why isn't he here, why doesn't he take a plane."

Far away in the cemetery a new funeral began. Someone went up to the faucet and tightened it. But the water went on leaking. Purple berets streamed between marble headstones on their way to the plot.

Close to her someone explained to the person sitting next to her: "Giora is his brother. He's the one who persuaded the boy to join a combat unit."—"And where is he, the brother?"—"In Boston. Something to do with computers."

The father collapsed into an armchair. Nobody went up to him. In the kitchen door a second cake made its appearance.

"Where's his wife?" [   ] asked someone in a black skull-cap sitting next to her. From the look on his face she realized that she wasn't here and she wasn't coming. Perhaps she was already dead herself. Perhaps they were divorced. Perhaps she too was in Boston, she thought, perhaps Giora had taken her with him. The successful brother wanted her for himself. The thoughts ran around in her head.

A newspaper passed from hand to hand. Again and again they read the details of the incident on the main street of Hebron. "What were they doing there in the first place," said the "crazy uncle," who rose restlessly from his seat every few minutes, in a loud voice. "In the middle of the Kasbah of Hebron, the Promised

Land of the Kasbah, right?" They looked at him with pity mingled with loathing. Pity he didn't leave with his sister. The "crazy uncle" got up and went to the toilet. On his white T-shirt was a printed picture of a dog, the head of a dog peeping over the top of a mountain or a wall, with a yellow sky above. Suddenly he stood still, and looked around at all the mourners. Nobody looked back at him except for her. Her eyes met the eyes of the dog.

What could she say. Ask if he was their child? If he was adopted? How could she put such a question? She said to someone in a casual tone, "And his parents, do they know already?" He stared at her for a minute and said, "What?"

"He's adopted, isn't he?" she whispered, where she got the nerve she had no idea. And the man said, "Oh, them. Of course they know. I wouldn't be surprised if they notified them before they notified him," he said, and pointed his chin in the direction of the upside-down television, where a man and a woman were standing side by side, with a little boy holding a glass of juice. The little boy sensed her staring at him and turned to look at her.

[   ] stood up and walked past them. She went up to the father lying on the armchair. She stood next to his bare feet, dirty with sand. She called his name. He didn't answer. In his restless sleep he muttered to her. Esther, Esther. What will become of us, Esther, what will become of us.

EMILE–YOEL

Emile walked out of the café to the street. From where he was sitting inside, Yoel looked at him, he didn't take his eyes off him, groping for his glass, staring. After a year had passed friends said to him, "Take him out a bit," "Buy him a dog." "A dog?" repeated the baffled Yoel. "Buy me a little dog," Emile begged, "a cat."

And Yoel was alarmed, because he understood that Emile didn't want to buy but to adopt, from the Society for the Protection of Animals, that is. The word was adopt but he said "buy." You want to adopt, Yoel wanted to say to him, as if this was a terrible thing. To adopt, that's what you want, right? And he thought of a big bitch, and of taking her pups. And of her bite. Teeth tearing flesh.

And there was a compromise, they went to sit in a café and on the way they bought a toy dog. And Emile stopped from time to time with the dog, which wagged its tail, and said something to it, and pointed to the heap of dead leaves. Yoel thought, "We have time." On one of the heaps collected by the street sweeper not long before was a small red fruit. Shed by some tree. And Emile explained to the dog, serious and confidential, "There's a tomato here. That's not good." The dog burrowed into the leaves.

Emile would stroke the cats in the street by the café and introduce them to his black dog and hold out his paw and his soft nails carefully, and Yoel watched them and he had the thought that perhaps the roles had been reversed, and Emile, aged seven and a half, was responsible for him, Yoel. You, he thought, can't stroke a cat, you can't lie on a heap of dry leaves. He can. He's well. His wound was deep but it's already healed. Without him you would . . . waitresses put hot chocolate and knives down next to him.

"It's for him," he raised his head and pointed.

And the waitress stood over Yoel's head. They looked together at the child holding his hand out to the cats. The dog lay at his feet, dozing. She wanted to say to him, "I heard about what happened to your wife." But she didn't say anything. Like everyone in the café, like everyone in the neighborhood, she knew the story in detail. She wanted to say, "You must be very sad." She said, "Careful he doesn't catch cold." She wanted to say, "It must be hard for you and the boy." She said, "I'll call him in, sit, sit, don't trouble yourself."

Emile drank the hot chocolate. There were cat hairs on his shirt and his hands and on the dog's fur. Yoel wiped the remnants of the cats off of his son. He wiped his hands, his shirt. He passed the palm of his hand over Emile and brushed his hair, his back. Emile laughed at the tickling. And then he hugged him a little. A lot.

Two cats looked for him through the glass of the café. But they saw only their reflections.

And it was perhaps then that Yoel thought for the first time, as he cleaned Emile up, of the idea that he immediately dismissed as complete nonsense. Disgraceful, he thought, you call yourself a father? But immediately, out of the same thoughts, pain and panic, perhaps, if I'm already gone, after all I'm nearly forty now, and who knows, he already knew two men who'd had heart attacks at around that age. Emile's laughter rose higher and higher. There has to be somebody else to worry and clean, to brush off the hairs. And to take him in. No, not today, and not tomorrow. But one needs to think of the future.

He had long black curls. His body, what can you say about a child's body? He was small. With one hand you could embrace him and there'd still be room left.

The years began to pass. Every year he had to have new shoes. In summer—sandals.

Emile had a green shirt with a picture of a lion. He had a Steve Austin shirt. And once he imagined how they took her out of the elevator and Oscar Goldman said, we can rebuild her, we have the technology, and they replaced half her body and an eye.

In winter he wore boots. The sweater Leah knitted him Yoel put away in the storage space above the ceiling, in a plastic bag, with mothballs. And the bag with the sweater in it he put into another bag. In days to come Emile would open those bags. Many days to come. Many many days until that distant opening. That strong smell.

There are a lot of things you could say about a child of seven years and one month. You could describe taking him to have his hair cut. In Levy's barbershop.

They put him on a board resting on the arms of the big chair.

The father sits at the back and reads the newspaper. Or, in the case of Yoel Zisu, he holds the newspaper as if he's just about to begin to read it, but in fact he's looking in the mirror. "Supervising the haircut."

And once Yoel looked in the mirror and didn't see himself. And he went into a big panic. But afterward it turned out that it wasn't a mirror but a glass window. They'd made a mistake when they installed it.

The child closes his eyes, sometimes tight, when the barber tells him to, so the hair won't get in his eyes.

The child remembers the dialogue between the barber and his father. The barber asks, "Should I use a razor," and the father replies, "What? No-no, no."

"What? No-no, no," instead of plain "no."

The child remembers the sheet around his neck and the moment they loosen the sheet and the soft brush begins to caress him. His face, his nose, his nape, his head. As if the child was a path and someone was sweeping him with a soft, soft broom.

And then a cloud of scent and you have to hold your breath.

And then a "few corrections," and the tips of the scissors, like a bird's beak, cut the air.

The child remembers the father's hand smoothing the cropped hair as soon as they walk out of the barbershop into the street. Only then the father inspects the haircut. So as not to pressure the barber, make him think he was being examined. He makes haste to pay him and leave.

And sometimes there's another little boy there, on the next chair, with another barber working on his hair, and their eyes meet in the depths of the mirror.

The strange feeling of being in the street with his hair cut short. Like coming out of the shower straight into the yard. As if not you but some other child had just stepped out. A kind of relief. There's a lot of happiness in having your hair cut.

The child remembers the big dustpan with the cut hair and curls in it, mixed with hair from other customers. Sometimes gray hair touched the hair of little children. And he remembers the soft broom, moving soundlessly over the barbershop floor, in the hands of the barber's nephew, whose name, he thinks, was then Chaim.

"Chaim, bring me some dry towels,"
"Chaim, take fifty from him,"
"Chaim, I need this kid shampooed."

And the child remembers coming home and his father saying to him, Go and have a shower and give your hair a thorough shampooing. To get rid of all the little hairs. And he says that he already had a shampoo in the barbershop. He remembers the hot water, his head in the hollow ("Just like the guillotine, eh?" Amikam Zisu once said when he took Yoel to the barber's, in the forties), the lathered hands, the strong jet on his scalp, and the towel wrapped round his head. "There you go, young man." And then the towel whipped off. Slamming the air. Like a flag. Like shutters flung open.

The child clearly remembers standing opposite the bathroom mirror, naked but with his head and the edge of the window caught in the reflection. It's him. It's him.

When he dies," Chaim whispered to him once, "I'll be the barber here. **I'll** be the one who cuts the hair." And Emile looked at him questioningly, and Chaim said, "He cuts your hair too short. It doesn't suit you." And Emile thought for a minute and whispered back, a promise, "I'll come to you to have my hair cut then too."

EMILE

And because the child was brown, and because his mother was killed at an early age, everybody assumed that his dead mother had been brown like him, since his father was white and thin and totally Ashkenazi. Thus they imagined her, teachers, parents of friends, the friends themselves, the social services personnel, the school principal, the gym teacher: brown, a little like him, lying crushed at the bottom of the pit, black hair, clothes, closed black eyes.

Emile walked, trampling cardboard boxes spread out like mattresses, the bedding of the homeless. Broken and mended cars squatted in the garages like caged lions.

"Black mother," he remembered someone once writing on a piece of paper, sticking it on his back. Years ago. Some things don't leave you.

He walked past a garage and recoiled, because through the slot for letters cut in the tin shutter, lowered at this hour of night, he glimpsed eyeglasses glinting. Someone was knocking from inside the garage, as if they were calling him. He stopped, heard a voice. Hello, hello there . . . hello? I'm locked in here, can you call somebody? You're a godsend, I've been yelling here for hours . . . Come here, have you got a cell phone on you? Can you pass it to me in here for a minute? And Emile said, no, no, certainly not, I haven't got one, they'll come and let you out tomorrow, and the voice said, tomorrow? today's Thursday, I'll be stuck here till Sunday . . . You're killing me here, go and get somebody, what am I going to do here all weekend long, don't be a bastard. And Emile said, still from a distance, okay, who do you want me to call, give me a number, I'll look for a public phone, I haven't got a cell phone, and the voice said, stop that bullshit, help me, what's the matter with you, call somebody, don't go, don't leave me, send someone to get me out of here, what numbers do you want from me, what public phones, can't you see I'm locked in here? Come closer, I can hardly hear you, I'll give you money, go get me something to eat, bring me something to drink, come here, you're killing me, I'm choking here, with the stink from the grease, I'll give you money, this is a mechanic's garage, I'm standing on a radiator, I'm going to fall in a minute, I'm going to break my neck . . . my legs are useless, matchsticks, like a cripple's, like I'm paralyzed, I work all day here under the cars, my leg's all twisted up, lying on my back all day under the bellies of the cars . . . I haven't seen the sun for two weeks now . . . my wife says I haven't got a vitamin in my body . . . the grease gets into the skin . . . they took my son away . . . I have a daughter too, in Canada . . .

Stinking smoke escaped from the slot in the shutter. Strong

cigarettes, inferior tobacco. And at that moment Emile knew for certain that it was his father locked in there. Yes, his real father. But of course he was wrong.

YOEL–EMILE

And one day Emile came home from the army, and Yoel, who didn't expect him, raised his eyes from the newspaper and raised his eyebrows in surprise. And Emile came in and said, "I've been discharged," and Yoel saw that the boy was indeed wearing civvies. Let's see: he was drafted on Monday. Today, if I'm not mistaken, it's Thursday. And Yoel said, "Already," and hid his face behind the newspaper. But the trembling of the big sheet of paper gave him away. And Emile said, "I got an exemption on grounds of unsuitability," and Yoel said, "What's that," and Emile said, "Three days in the army," and laughed a rather forced laugh. And Yoel stood up and threw down his newspaper and ground it into the floor with his foot. Emile was alarmed. But Yoel laughed reassuringly. The phone rang. They didn't answer it. Why didn't they answer? Because they went to the beach.

And he thought that he should talk to him now, at this important moment in their lives, about the whole business of the adoption, and about the years that had passed, but he knew that it was impossible to "talk" because there was too much to talk about. He couldn't contain the joy of Emile's early release. A gift of life. There was also a whisper of shame, of worry, what would the neighbors say, the people at work. But this voice died down, and a brightly colored Venetian carriage and golden light and the singing of gondoliers was heard. And a bell. Released, released, released, released. He won't be killed. He won't kill. It won't happen.

And he felt that he had done her will. That she was sitting here, close, perhaps at the foot of the lifeguard's tower, hidden behind a very wide-brimmed straw hat, leaning back in relief. And looking at the sea. At last she can lean back. And he actually heard her say it. At long last I can lean back. Only now he understood how heavy the weight had been. How much tension had accumulated in his body, like a spring coiled up inside him. Held down. His shoulders were stiff. His fear that the child would be forced to shoot a child. His fear that the child would beat someone. And Yoel didn't care if he died, if Emile was wounded—that is, preferably not, of course, preferably not! To be killed at the age of eighteen, what good was that? Yet you had to die sometime. To kill was something different. To live a whole lifetime without killing a single human being, that was wonderful. There's a chance of living a decent life. Along comes the army and takes away that bare minimum of decency. You kill or you help others to kill. Even in the radio station they help to kill, even in the recruiting center.

And he had that dream of giving Emile to a Palestinian family to adopt, in Ramallah. And when they come from the recruiting center he'd say to them, no, he'd notify them, officially, that the child belonged to "the minorities." And the recruiting officers would ask in disappointment, "What, he's an Arab?"

They looked at the waves. There was a kind of line between the waves and the shore drawn by children with plastic rakes.

Yoel said, "Now, that this burden has been lifted," Emile said nothing. What would he do tomorrow? Two weeks ago he was still in school. And then this military interregnum, like a dream in a three-day-long sleep, at the end of which you wake up, hot and dazed, and go to the mirror, and are no longer sure of anything, perhaps you were changed into somebody else while you were sleeping.

When he left the classroom, the last of the students after the last matriculation exam, the school was already drained and empty, listless with the end-of-the-year listlessness, and the teachers' cars had already driven off on their way to the spas and the resorts and the pleasure cruises, and the chairs were already stacked on the desks in all the classrooms until the next year, which would come after the long summer which had only just begun, and the blackboards were clean and wet, like the well-swept floors, and in the lab the long test tubes were quiet, and in the gym the air escaped little by little from the balls, and the basketball courts were empty and full of silence. And Emile walked around and looked for a while at the high school where he had spent the last four years, the school of whose burden he had wished to rid himself every single day, and which now looked to him like an abandoned, beloved home. And he tried to conjure up memories of his high-school years, but from the big gate behind him the deputy principal rattled his keys and then banged them on the mesh, calling him, holding the gate open a little, a moment before locking it.

A goal presented itself. They stood up, shook their towel, drove to the cemetery. They hadn't been there for a long time. They stood next to the grave. And the smell of the sea seeped out of their clothes onto the graves. Here lies. 1937–1976. Like then, a dozen years ago, when they stood there, in exactly the same place, surrounded by many mourners. The sound of the Kaddish prayer rose from an adjacent plot, and Emile pricked up his ears to listen. And he also whispered "Amen" with his eyes closed. Yoel poured some water on the stone and cleaned it with the squeegee from the car.

Suddenly there are fresh flowers in their hands. Emile went up to the big faucet. The water splashed into the olive tin. The wire handle hurt his hand. Yoel whispered into the noise of the water from behind him, "I rescued the child, Leah." Even though it wasn't him who had done the rescuing.

Emile looked at the rows of military graves on the other side of the path. His eyes filled all at once with stinging tears and his throat closed up. Because he knew that his place was there. That he should have been. That he definitely would have been killed. And he knew this beyond a shadow of a doubt. That the army had intended him to die. To get rid of him. That if he had remained in basic training he too would have been buried here. Maybe tomorrow. Very soon. And Yoel would have skipped from grave to grave and shared one bunch of flowers between them.

I would definitely have been killed there," Emile said to him and raised the tin of water a little. And Yoel replied, "You're right."

Yoel held the tin of water from the bottom. Together they tilted it into the cracked marble vase. And onto the letters.

The father held these words back: I dreamed that you were burned in a tank. The tin was completely empty.

They sat on the ground next to the grave. And they wanted to weep and weep. Yoel reached out his right hand and put it on Emile's cropped head.

Under their knees, deep but not very deep, Leah Zisu's skeleton rested in a spotless, disintegrating shroud. And a little deeper lay the ground water and molten rocks, and deeper still it was impossible to see. A man came up to them and silently requested the tin for his flowers.

YOEL–LEAH–EMILE

After they returned from the cemetery, and after the last of the condolence callers had taken their leave, gone downstairs, made their way home, and turned on the television, yawning in front of the screen but needing to lighten the oppression of the graveyard a little, and the child left with his father, not even seven years old, the rage welled up in Yoel for the first time, the bitter anger. All kinds of things and thoughts rose up in him. Among them the fact that from now on it was all on him. It's all on me, he thought. It's all on me. And he didn't even know how to make a sandwich for school. And what to do if the child had a fever. And what size trousers he wore. And his homeroom teacher's name. And what time he got out of school every day. And he was part of a club that flew model airplanes, where did this activity take place? What toothpaste did he need? Where was his vaccination card? All of that had been on her. Now you have to learn everything, he thought.

He didn't want to learn. He didn't want to know anything.

The first night he dreamed that someone was calling him to

go back to high school. And as soon as he went back the principal yelled at him for moving a desk. And this was forbidden. He hadn't known. But he was too proud to tell the principal. So they beat him severely, threw him downstairs, all this happened at school, and they buried him in the library.

The problem was that he thought that this wasn't "his life." That "his life" had been when she was still alive. And there was the child. That was okay. That was right. But Leah's death? No. That he refused to accept into his life. Like a picture someone gives you and you're not prepared to hang it up but you can't throw it out either. He was ready to be with Emile a little every day after work. But not **all** day. No no, he thought. Not that. That was out of the question. And he expected someone to come and relieve him of this weight. So he could go back to living like before. A simple life. In the morning at the office, planning roads and bypasses and interchanges. At midday—lunch. At half past five he left everything, took the number 7 bus that passed there at five forty. Rode four stops and before six he was already home. For this he was ready.

A religious man at work told him that if the moon didn't revolve round the earth we would veer off our orbit, the system would become unstable, and in the end we would slide into the gravitational pull of the sun and fall into it and be burned up. It's like a balancing weight, he said. And Yoel said impatiently, why are you telling me this? And the religious man said, your moon has been taken away from you.

In days to come he understood that the moon hadn't been taken away from him, the moon had been replaced.

But it would take a hard six months for the moon to shine again in his life. That is to say, for it to be revealed, this moon that was not covered by a cloud and nevertheless did not shine. That is to say, it shone, it shone, but Yoel did not perceive its light.

*　　*　　*

The last of the condolence callers left. It was the sixth day of the seven-day mourning period. On the next day, the seventh day, no one would come. Yoel slammed the bathroom window shut and flushed the toilet. He opened the door. Emile was sitting there, leaning against the wall and reading a comic. And the boy raised his eyes to him and said, "I need to go too." And Yoel said, "Why didn't you say so, I would have come out sooner," and then he added, "The paper's finished, I'll get another roll," and he took down the brown cardboard cylinder in order to throw it away. "What are you reading there," he asked. And in order to make the child laugh he looked at him through the brown cardboard cylinder.

Emile raised his head from the comic and looked at his father as if he was seeing through him into the bathroom. He didn't laugh. And Yoel seemed to be caught in Emile's glazed stare. And so they froze for a moment facing one another other. Until Yoel shook himself and turned back in order to reopen the window. And then he saw it, lying on the shelf, a pink and red box of tampons.

YOEL–LEAH–EMILE

He put on the record with Beethoven's cello sonatas. Played by Jacqueline du Pre and Daniel Barenboim. The sonatas had been recorded in Edinburgh in 1970, and Yoel and Leah were present at the concert.

"They're married, you know," he said and turned the record over.

"So are we," she replied from the armchair behind him as he was bending over the gramophone.

He turned to look at her, waiting for the sounds, her eyes were closed, her head tilted back against the armchair. The whisper of the needle on the record came over the speakers. And it seemed that the cello would never be heard, the piano would never be heard, only this whisper, like messages from very remote cultures, broadcasting their histories over ancient radio waves, recorded by sensitive instruments.

They were at that concert. They didn't even know that it

was being recorded. Was Emile there? No. Emile was then in [   ]'s belly in Jaffa, and he didn't hear those sounds. But in the days to come he would hear the record.

The cough you can hear there in the first part of the sonata in G minor, after about five and a half minutes, is Yoel. It was a bad winter. He'd been sent to a conference on sunken roads in Scotland. And Leah hadn't wanted want to stay home alone. And he caught the flu.

With every second, as the music progressed, the knowledge of their failure as a couple bore in on them. They would never have a child. Thirty-three years old, and the spring had already been stopped by a stone. And they wanted one very much. They even knew what they would call him: Gil. And the disappointment of their four parents. Somebody sneezed, others echoed his cough. There was a kind of flu epidemic in Scotland then, in 1970. But Jacqueline du Pre and Daniel Barenboim were absorbed in their playing, and apparently didn't notice the noise. Only they were healthy in a hall full of sick people, thought Leah. And Yoel thought that it was precisely for these coughs that the music came. In order to heal them, to be there by their side, to nurse them, not to let the noise and the coughing prevail. It was a severe winter in Scotland, and the sick people got out of bed and came in spite of everything to hear the couple, to hear Beethoven. And indeed, the music cured them completely.

And after a few years the record came out, and Leah bought it for Yoel for his thirty-seventh birthday. When he woke up he looked at the sunlight penetrating the curtains, muttered "Hih . . . hih . . . "

and paused for two seconds, shouted and sneezed noisily. In the middle of the sonata he fell asleep, on the armchair. The record came to an end. And Leah was no longer in the room.

Saturday afternoon. There was no hurry to go anywhere. He rose from the armchair. Padded on bare feet to the bed. Behind the door of the little room he heard her saying something to the child. He let his hand rest on the door handle for a moment. Strained his ears to listen to their conversation filtered through the door. His fingers hovered over the handle:

* * *

In the mirror his face appeared to him. The closed door. A tip of light. Leah stood and looked at him looking. A child of four. He pointed at his reflection. He said, "That's not me." She was dismayed, she didn't know what to do. They said, we won't tell him till he's six. But in a little while she would tell him.

Yoel heard snatches of talk.

Four years ago. Four years? Four years. Your father and I. We went to Scotland. No, in an airplane. It was cold there. Did it snow? No. Like now? No. Cold. Cold. And we were at a concert. They played lovely music. On the cello. What's a cello?

Did you leave me with Grandpa Amikam? No. With who then?

We couldn't . . . we couldn't give birth to you by ourselves then. What about today? Today? Can you today? You . . . couldn't fit me inside? Yes. You could say that. That we couldn't fit you in. In your tummy? Here?

But we wanted. Only you. We wanted to hug you already. So we went. Together? Together. Somewhere else. Where they give. Where we could get you.

We went inside. And we said, where's Emile? There's a child waiting for us here. He . . . Me? You.

You were there. You had been born yesterday. Yesterday from then. You had two sets of . . . Mommy-Daddies. No, I don't know who. We're not allowed to know. No. And not their names either. They . . . I don't know why. They couldn't take responsibility for a child. Maybe . . . because they were . . . Wounded? Wounded. Sick. They loved you. Of course they did. But they couldn't. It happens sometimes that people want to but it's too hard. Did they freeze? In the cold? No no, they weren't in Scotland, let me explain . . .

So they said to us, you take him. To us. Yes. He's yours. We love him. We love you.

No, there was no need to fit you inside. You were already out.

No, you didn't have teeth yet.

Yes. It's you. For sure. It's you. Like you were then.

It's me too. Us. Yes.

Look. There's room for both of us in the mirror. Move up a bit.

Yes. Yes. Together, yes. Forever. Forever.

No-no

No, no

YOEL

After Leah's death he embarked on the road of death. He would go into a restaurant and forget to pay. He would meet old acquaintances and forget their names. "Who are you," he frequently asked. "Yes, that's all very well," he said, "but **who are you**."

Was he putting on an act? Did he want to hurt them? With the child things were a little better during that first half year. There was hardly any discernable difference. As if, vis-à-vis the child, there was a piece of the old Yoel left, enough to make normal life possible. But sometimes he would look at the child as though Emile were a heavy parcel someone had left behind, or stolen goods given you by a friend to hand on, and you know you're going to get caught, and you'd throw it out and run away if you only could.

He only had a few such moments. Each of them could be measured in seconds. Dark seconds, during which he hated Emile for being Emile. For his very existence. You've been screwed, he thought. You did a good deed, you took in a child for adoption, and what happened? Now he's a millstone round your neck. And you, like a donkey, spend all day circling the stone. That's the kind of image that came into his head. For a few seconds. A few seconds of dripping poison, and already all your veins are black, your blood murky, your soul sinks and turns into motor oil.

His soul turned into black oil. If they put it into a car the car would run. Go uphill. Downhill. He had this thought. And he wanted to tell it to someone. This insight about the car. But who could he tell? Perhaps Emile himself?

His elderly parents would call, he wouldn't answer their questions. Only "yes" and "no" and for the most part silence. Questions that he couldn't answer with yes or no he wouldn't answer at all. And most of the questions fell into this category. They invited him for big meals. They had a cook. But the lids stayed on the pots there, in Yoel's parents' home, and their contents got cold. And eggplants burst in the oven.

But when Emile came home Yoel would put a kind of mask of normality on his face, and hold it tight, so it wouldn't suddenly fall off and reveal who was really there.

And at the office he presented plans for a bridge. To you and me it would have looked fine. But if anyone had built that bridge there would have been a terrible disaster. Lucky they didn't build it. Or perhaps they did?

He set out on the road of death. The Earth had slipped into a dangerous new gravitational field. From day to day the sun grew bigger, redder, and more swollen. After four months the edges of the planet began to char. Local fires spread through the atmosphere.

She wouldn't let him leave. She sent threads. Webs. Cables. She sent his elevator down. Further and further. Floor after floor. Her hands were strong.

And once he picked up another woman. Saw her in the street and approached her. And she was a nasty piece of work. A real bitch. She, for example, gave her son medicine even when there was no need. Without a prescription. She, for example, when her garbage spilled onto the stairs, didn't go back to clean it up. She, for example, liked to send smoke into the apartment of the elderly couple above her. Stuck her hand outside so the smoke would rise up and through their window. She, for example, thought that the whole business of peace with the Egyptians was a very bad thing. That war was only natural. In order to thin out the superfluous people. And there were plenty of those. She, for example, also hated reading Hebrew literature. She also hated all women poets. She thought that if a woman was a poet she had to be a nympho-maniac. Or a whore. She also once ran over a cat. A kitten. She also liked to eat red meat. She also wore lipstick that shone in the dark like a red, talking traffic light. She also called every second woman in the street "a little cocksucker." She had elderly parents, she couldn't stand them. But the inheritance, etc., etc.

Yoel sat opposite her in a café. He listened to her talk. He felt an urgent need to go to bed with her. She saw the way he was looking at her breasts. "The guy wants to eat me alive," she thought. "Everybody wants to eat me alive." And she asked him, "So did you lose something down there?"

They went to her apartment, and Yoel looked at her when she took off her clothes. And he was filled with a great, powerful desire to break something upon her. To pick up a vase and bring it down on her head. Or to take a swing at her with a metal chair and bend it out of shape. She looked at him and said, "You're horny as a goat, Giora."

"Gershon," that's what he'd told her his name was. And she changed it to "Giora" by mistake. "So why don't you take off your clothes." The phone rang. He fell on her. He pushed her onto the bed. He didn't let her answer the phone.

She had silver stars on her nail polish. On her toenails too.

LEAH–YOEL

On that morning the phone rang an hour or so after she left the house. She took Emile to school and went to see how the builders were getting on in the building where they had purchased an apartment. The eighth floor. The last floor. The penthouse floor. And he answered impatiently, he didn't want to be bothered. But then he got scared, perhaps the child, perhaps he had split a nail, which had already happened once before.

They told him to come quickly. He recognized the address immediately.

The minutes after that he didn't remember. How he got dressed, even brushed his teeth, washed his face. Suddenly he was getting out of the taxi. Suddenly he was paying and not taking the change. Walking past the ambulance parked at the entrance to the building.

The next thing he remembered was standing by the open elevator. In the meantime they had already moved her out of the elevator. Two policemen were taking measurements and photographs. Someone shouted at them from the top of the shaft, and they, stretching their necks, shouted back. They shone a flashlight into the opening.

They had already taken her out. Laid her on the concrete floor.

Next to Leah's head were the police doctor's feet. He told him briefly what had apparently happened. He said that according to the policemen she had removed the red tape and entered the elevator. There was a notice saying that it was forbidden, apparently she hadn't seen it. In another few minutes they would have fixed it. The technician had just gone downstairs, she'd come by between shifts . . . and the doctor pointed to the technician, who was sitting with his back to them and smoking, rubbing his eyes with his free hand.

She died on the spot, he said sorrowfully. A blow like that, eight floors . . .

Yoel was shaking all over. Sit, sit, the doctor said to him.

And Yoel sat down and leaned against an unpainted concrete wall. From inside the elevator rose the sound of hammering, a policeman pounding on the crushed walls of the car with his iron flashlight.

Could it be a dream? he suddenly asked the doctor. Because he had already had such dreams before. Like the dream that he was traveling in a train and it turned out that the bridges had all exploded.

Yoel looked at her. She lay still on her back. They didn't have anything to cover her with. It looked as if nothing had happened to her. But she was frozen. He didn't know what to do or what to think. The child, he thought, the child's at school. He doesn't know anything. Yoel imagined hearing the bell for recess.

And the doctor said, they'll take her away in a minute. Perhaps you'd like to say good-bye to her. And he held out his hand to pull him to his feet.

Yoel approached fearfully. Everybody else stepped back. The policemen came out of the elevator and switched off their big flashlight. Only then Yoel noticed that the elevator technician was handcuffed. It looked as if somebody had hit him in the face.

Yoel went and stood next to her. He kneeled at her side. He touched her cheek with trembling, quaking fingers.

And then her lips parted. She said something. A kind of long "maaaa." Yoel was struck dumb. And then he screamed. Everyone looked at each other. The younger policeman was horrified. The older policeman came up to Yoel.

She said something, he said. She said something, she called me.

The doctor bent over the body. He checked its pulse. Palpated its arteries. He shook his head at the inquiring policeman.

"Leah! Leah!" Yoel shouted close to her ear. "Leah! Leah! Show me a sign that you can hear me. Tell me what you said to me, tell me what you said to me."

The doctor put his hand on Yoel. Squeezed his shoulder and shook it. It was very painful. He felt as if his shoulder had been dislocated. He shouted, it hurts, it hurts. But the doctor went on shaking and squeezing. Harder and harder.

On the fourth floor twelve Palestinian plasterers sat still on the concrete floor. The plaster in their pails hardened. And their tools lay scattered over the apartment.

In front of the building the doors of the ambulance stood open.

THE CITY

The eye looks at the place where there were once the sun, the moon, the city, and all the stars, the Earth, Venus, Mars, etc. And there's nothing there. Right, left, nothing. Everything has disappeared. Black and empty. It can't be, but it is. There's nothing. At first it burned, the sun, a revolving furnace in the blue sky. Then it swelled, burned everything around it. Afterward it shrank. Collapsed into itself. It stopped shining. And without the light, without the heat, there's nothing. The eye searches, but in vain. Hands go out, grope, maybe there's a light switch, maybe a curtain will be parted, and everything will suddenly be returned. Like at night. When you wake up and your left arm is numb and frozen, a cold, dead roll of rubber. And you try, with your right hand, to touch the cold flesh, but the right hand too seems to have disappeared. And you want to scream. And you scream.

EMILE–YOEL

Other years arrived. The music petered out. And children's light coats hung in closed closets summer and winter. The child grew, he no longer sent notes, drew pictures of love. And summer and winter and fall. Almost every year they had to buy a new coat, and new shoes. At the age of sixteen Emile went to a Waterboys concert and when he came home his breath stank. A year later a girlfriend appeared. They would shut themselves in his room, and Emile would emerge from time to time like a cat slinking through the house. To take something to eat. To throw a shirt into the washing machine. To drink. She too, the girlfriend, would come out from time to time. And once she passed obliquely in her panties and Yoel shuddered, and buried his face in his thick book.

And Emile would go to her place when her parents weren't at home. Disappear for two or three days at a time. And Yoel would sit alone in the kitchen, looking at the trees swaying in the wind, or at the neighbors. And they would see him looking and pull down their blinds. Slowly the whole world closed around him. He would leave the office early as his fiftieth birthday approached. And there was a sense of "that's it," of great weariness, and a powerful urge to travel and to sleep for a long time and not to wake up.

Emile needed a blood transfusion. And they tested Yoel. And there was no problem. His blood matched. And so the two of them lay on two beds, side by side, with thin tubes transferring blood from one to the other.

No. No. You have to tell the truth, he thought. They tested Yoel, and it turned out that he couldn't donate. He couldn't give. A rare blood type. AB. So he stood facing the nurse in charge and begged, as if it was up to her. She retreated in embarrassment to the shelf of syringes. All the donors looked at him in astonishment. With all the tubes. And all the test tubes. And all those cookies they handed out to strengthen them, so they wouldn't collapse when they got off the bed.

And when Emile recovered, two or three months later, Yoel asked him hesitantly if he could go away for a while on a trip. And Emile, who was still weak, took out his earphones and said, "Go ahead, Dad, it's no big deal." But Emile felt a pang of anxiety too, and that night he dreamed: his father is going abroad and arrives at a hotel, and they tell him, everything's fine, it's an excellent hotel, and the hotel has its own chickens and every morning he'll get a fresh, warm egg, there's only one problem, but he shouldn't let it bother him, and he asks, what's the problem, and they say, you'd better see for yourself, and he goes up to his room, walks down carpeted corridors, someone carries his suitcase and someone else holds a huge candlestick with a candle stuck in it to light the way, and a third person opens the door of the room with an old-fashioned iron key, and there, in the room, in the light of the candle, he sees a dwarf, a child of eight or nine, but pale and bald, and they say to him, he's sleeping in the room with you.

EMILE

Those years came round. When Emile wouldn't respond to him. When he went into his room and didn't come out until his father was asleep. And once Yoel had to go and get him out of jail. And there were all kinds of voices on the phone. He was seventeen, and the age of eighteen was approaching. The dangerous age. The terrifying age. The age of "opening the file." Yoel had no idea. And Emile already had it all planned. He marked his birthday on the calendar. He would go in the next day. The next day. Get up at six. Or five. He already knew where to go. He would take all the documents. Leah's death certificate too, which he had once found under his father's radio, and taken possession of. He would take pictures of himself as a child. He would take the lock of hair his mother had cut off before his first haircut and put in an envelope. He would take the drawing of the angel. He would pack it all up, and go to the bureau. And there they would authenticate him. Take his fingerprints. Maybe take blood. Let them do whatever they have to. I'm even prepared to sleep there. But in the end they

184

would open the file. And he imagined it again and again. How the official—he knew exactly what he would look like—would study the file and raise his head and look at Emile. And again up and down. Like the policemen holding your passport at the airport. In the end there would be no doubt, and the file would be stamped. And a few seconds would pass. How would it happen? Would the official copy the names on a piece of paper and hand it to him? Would they let him read the original file? And what would he see there? Photographs? Of who? Would the file be thick? Would it have a rubber band round it? Would there be a letter that somebody—his parents—had left for him, eighteen years ago? Would he read the letter at once, in front of the official? Would he leave the room? Where would he read it? And what if he couldn't make out the handwriting? Or perhaps his parents would already be waiting for him there, behind the counter? Behind a screen he didn't notice at first, and then, suddenly, their shoes would peep out? And the official would ask, "May I call them over? Are you sure? I'm bringing them in, now, is that definitely what you want?" And Emile would nod, and he would press a kind of button on the wall, and a door would open? And then what? Was there some kind of restaurant there especially for meetings like these? Would he shake their hands? Or kiss them? Would he be able to touch them at all? He opened the datebook. And he knew when he'd been born. He'd checked. Soon he'd be seventeen and a half. It was another six months. Maybe they were waiting for him there, and they would go on waiting, and there would be no need for any procedures? They would simply see him, and they would recognize him, and they would embrace him calmly, and they would simply leave together? But maybe they were violent, maybe they would hit him? Hurl insults at him? Were they shorter than him, he wondered in horror—are they shorter than me already?

[   ]

Very close to a big cactus thorn, the skin of her fingers. On the stairs, on a hot day at the end of October, the shade was cool and the roar of the traffic on the nearby expressway sounded like the noise of the air conditioner pervading a dreamer's sleep. And as always she was drawn to the pain. Touching a live wire. Touching a hot iron so as to let the scream out.

There was nobody near. The gardeners were already taking their afternoon nap in the gardeners' shed, snoring underneath the calendars of previous decades, naked women who had greatly aged since those days. The city seemed to have vanished in the blink of an eye, as if she had left the atmosphere and all at once everything had become empty and still. The chirping of birds she had up till now only read about in books, and the low murmur of cactuses curled up in beds, basking in the sun, turning toward her as if to say something, or to prick her, or bite. And there were names of plants on little notices, "Kalanchoe Humbert" next to "Kalanchoe Millotti" and "Velvety Kalanchoe," plants she had never heard of, and here, in the garden, the little botanical labels were like the titles of kings and counts. A red train drove through the cactuses, she never imagined it was so close.

If only I could lie here for hours, she thought, disappear, dip deeper and deeper into this bath of shade. I have stepped into a trap, she thought. And then she tried to remember the moment, making love then, in Eilat, the moment when the child they had called Emile was created. When it had happened was clear. The date was even written down somewhere on a tattered piece of paper. But she didn't remember either the day or the time or the place or the pleasure. Only pain and panic came immediately to mind. And out of them you were born.

She entered the hothouse. She thought to herself, I can hide here. They close at three, and I'll hide at half past two, there's hardly anybody here, and nobody would suspect that anyone would want to stay. The gardeners will go home and close up and I'll be here all night. And if I'm hungry I'll find fruit in the orchard. And if I'm thirsty I'll drink the water from the sprinklers. And if I'm cold I'll go back inside the hothouse. Just one night. As she had already done a few times before. Usually nobody found her. But once in Haifa somebody saw her lying between the flowerbeds and called the police.

She pulled her cell phone out of her bag and switched it off, and then she removed the battery and suddenly threw it over her shoulder, into the bushes. And she regretted it immediately. But the thorns stretched out their hands and wouldn't let her get it back. There was only this desire to be outside of the city, and the garden was a good place. A place where Yoel Zisu couldn't come, like today, and beg, and plead, and ooze guilt. Touch her with his fingers. Give her little drawings. Shout at the walls in her house.

And already she imagined the phone calls trying to breach the thorns and reach her. He'll get hold of your number and phone. But she had switched it off. "Mimosa Pubica," she pronounced aloud. A child was created in you, and now here you are, after thirty-eight years. A huge disruption. But we're all alive. Close, very close, almost touching, but there's still a veil. She saw the stitches. And she saw him, Emile, through the window of a train that passed there, frozen as in a video on a vibrating "pause." He looked at her. No train passed. The trains were still far away, near the Acre station, in the north. They would never reach this place.

In the hospital. Emile was one day old. He had just been born. They were together for two hours. Or three. He tried to suck her nipple too. Once. All these years she hadn't remembered this. Now she suddenly remembered. His mouth. His fingernails.

She walked up a path to an open space, passing by the blind people's garden. In her imagination she saw the groping hands, the white canes among flowers and fleshy leaves, guide dogs dozing in the weak sunlight of this garden-within-a-garden. And she closed her eyes. They were there, all of them. She and her husband shutting himself up in his cupboard more and more from day to day, pouring water on his head, half his strings snapped, and Yoel Zisu, and the body of his wife whose name she didn't know, and also the child Emile, who suddenly broke up into all the children he had been, every year a child, every year an abandoned child, every day, every second, not one child she'd abandoned but millions. All of them.

And she saw them, all of them, yes, all five of them, passing and groping with their hands stretched out before them, seeking but not finding one another. Calling, close, nearly touching.

The path descended beneath her feet. A white butterfly passed between the thorns, and when it passed she discovered the poisonous plant. Surrounded by a low fence, and peeling black skulls on the fence. Like a sea anemone reaching for the air. The plant looked at her as it looked at everyone who saw it. And then it stiffened slightly. She came a little closer.

On a small stand were plaques memorializing the donors to the park. The plaques blinked in the strong sunlight, and Emile's mother read the names of the donors, already regretting the whole business, the battery she had recklessly thrown into the thorns, now she would have to buy a new one. At the end of the square stood a sign. She went up to read it. "Noah Naftolski Garden— Man of plants and flowers." And the words were suddenly terrible to her, like bad news, the worst, and she said to herself, oh no, oh no, man of plants and flowers, plants and flowers, plants and flowers. And then she said, suddenly, in a clear voice, Emile Suissa—child of plants and flowers. And she saw, with her own eyes, the name Emile Suissa engraved on the sign instead of the name Noah Naftolski, and on the memorial plaques she saw his name, over and over again. The park for the blind had been donated by Emile Suissa in memory of his parents Malka and Eliyahu Suissa. In memory of his parents Malka and Eliyahu Suissa. In memory of his parents. In memory of his parents. And she spoke to the sign, and the words had been stuck in her mouth for so many years, "It wasn't me who wanted to leave you there." It was him. It was him. It was him, she said to herself, just like then, when she'd suddenly wanted to go back, back to the child, and when he grabbed her by force, no, choked her, pulled her outside, dragged her along, and decent people looked at them, at this boy and girl, and wondered what to do and didn't do anything. And she kept quiet and stopped screaming because he bent her, pulled her, dragged her, nearly killed her. And she bit him and he absorbed the bite without a sound until he found a hiding place behind a storeroom full of hospital pajamas, and he said to her, Malka, one more scream like that and I'll kill you. I'll strangle you right here in the storeroom. What was the matter with her all of a sudden, what. And she kept quiet and nodded, weeping wordlessly. And then she tried to claw his face. Then he panicked and banged her head on the storeroom wall. And then he waited for her to wake up. A few minutes passed. When she woke up he said to her, It's over, some people took him, they'll take care of him now, it's finished. He said that he saw him being driven away in a big car. And when evening fell they left, by bus. They sat far apart. She took a seat behind the driver, and he went to the back of the bus. She saw him moving away into the depths of the mirror. Getting smaller. She never wanted to see him again. Not ever. Never. But in the end they stayed together.

[   ]

And one day, years later, a relation of his came to visit them. He phoned on short notice, said he was on his way. He'd just landed. With a suitcase and an umbrella. And she said to her husband, Your kin's coming. She didn't remember his name. And he looked at her. My kin? And she said to him: Yes. So he fell to the floor and fainted on the spot.

THE CITY

An old pickup truck. On a muddy path. A wide field. It hasn't stopped raining since yesterday evening. The noise of the wiper hitting the windshield. They can hardly see. And the noise of the rain. The drops shooting from the sky, striking. Big, strong drops. All of them on the open bed of the truck. Heavy clouds like rocks saturated with water. All five of them. The rain beats down, lashes them like whips, like needles, like a tempest. The pickup sways on the potholed path. The wiper barely succeeds in removing the heavy layer of water from the windshield. It battles, small, too slow, and again and again, again and again, the water covers the glass. They sit in the back, crowded, packed, glued together, one silently swaying mass. Coats, a muffler, a wooly hat. The cold. The rain beats against [   ]'s glasses. He gave up trying to wipe them with the sleeve of his coat long ago. His hat, a kind of crumpled beret, fits tight on his head. The rain collects in the creases of the beret, and runs down, like water in a gutter, to his ears, his cheeks, the white stubble covering his face, to the two grooves on the sides of his nose. It hits [   ]'s slightly open, gasping mouth. Her hands on her eyes, to keep them dry. But one little peek is enough to wet them again. And still she covers them, as if against the sun. But everything around them is completely gray. There is no sun. No shade. Only mud and the noise of the engine, and the noise of the suspension as they go over the potholes. When they hit a pothole they all get toppled at once. Cold stinging drops on the top of Yoel's head. His back to the rain, wrapped in a soaking wet blanket, he puts out his tongue every few seconds to taste the rain. His thinning hair is plastered to his forehead, there's no point in trying to fix it. Whenever the wheel he's sitting over hits a hole or a plank, he feels a sharp pain through his whole body, as if something is coming undone all at once, as if the plaster over his heart is being ripped off all at once. Leah leans against his side, her head falling forward, swaying, half awake, half asleep, burying her face in his neck, exposing her nape to protect her face. Behind her ears streams of water running down and getting into the gap between her collar and her neck. She tries to close this gap with her scarf, but it opens up over and over again in the strong wind, which the driver's cabin is too low to block. A flash of lightning illuminates the gray fields, and Emile, with a bit of cardboard covering his head, puts both hands over his ears and then buries them deep in the pockets of his old coat again, his back is wet, he's shivering, sick, there's water in his shoes, only his pockets are still dry. So his hands are too. The rain drives down at a slant, hitting them, hitting the path, splashing on the wheels, hitting the windows, hitting [   ]'s nose, getting into his nostrils with every breath, streaming onto his slightly parted lips, muttering something incessantly. Even if he yelled it would be impossible to hear. The whistling of the wind, the engine, the rain beating on the roof of the driver's cabin. It gets stronger and stronger. It will never, never, never stop. The drops begin to bounce, hail, as sharp as stones. It beats down, straight into [   ]'s ear, onto Yoel Zisu's temple, it hits Emile's knees, slowly melts his cardboard. But they won't let go. They won't let go of the cardboard. Even though the rain beats the wet ground in front of them, even though it turns the dirt road in front of them into a shallow river of mud. They go on, they go on, in the storm and fog, in the winter wind. Every gaping hole in the road, every stone in the wheel, every plank thrown across the way, every explosion of thunder, all the distant lighting bolts, the cold.

196

YOEL

When he looked for his passport he found the drawing along with other drawings and notes from Emile in an envelope with the words "From the child" written on it in pencil that had already faded. It was a drawing Emile had made very many years ago. Perhaps at the age of three. Who is it? Me? Maybe it's Leah. Suddenly it wasn't clear to him. Without a doubt he remembered Emile tearing a page out of a notebook and drawing the face in one go. Who is it, he thought fearfully. Who is it, is it her? Or is it me? Who is it, who is it?

Yoel's fingers drummed on the table, as if his fate depended on the answer to this question. He stared at the staring eyes. He examined the date on his airline ticket again. 7/7/07. The date seemed to tell him that he had to go, that it was right to go. He took out his passport and put the drawing in his shoulder bag. And suddenly he was seized by a shivering fit, as when your temperature suddenly drops and your whole body is bathed in sweat and a wet towel lies heavily on your forehead, and he thought, she's looking at me. And he remembered how one day he came home and went into the bedroom and lay down, and the angel, which had been hanging there for twelve years, was missing, and in its place there was only a kind of empty square, and a very rusty, crooked nail.

And the next day he was already sitting comfortably on his seat in the airplane. And in the plane he dreamed of someone flying to Italy, but he didn't stop when the plane landed, he traveled further north, past the lakes and onward, to Switzerland, to the snowy mountains, he would only reach the high peaks the following day, traveling all night, piano music in the car, and there he would get out of the car and look at the black empty alpine night, burying his hands in the pockets of the thick, coarsely woven coat his grandfather had once given him, when it was still far too big for him, and the child had hated the coat and its rough smell, and what was the old man thinking to give him a coat for his birthday, and his parents were embarrassed too, and hid the "rag" away somewhere, but today there isn't a winter's day when the child doesn't wear that coat, and in summer he travels to cold countries in order to wear it a little longer. And when he gives it to the laundry he stands in the door and waits.

Yoel opened his eyes. His feet were planted over the mountains of Crete. A meal was boiling on the tray in front of him. And he didn't have the faintest idea of who or where he was.

* * *

And it was already the last day of the trip. He sat on a step opposite the Duomo. He took out the book he thought he would read during the trip but didn't. He didn't want to be seen with a Hebrew book on the streets of Italy, it embarrassed him, he was afraid that he would be "identified." Now, a few hours before taking a taxi to the airport, he said to himself that he had to read a little. Otherwise why did you schlep the book all this way? Dragging books around as if God knows what. But instead of reading he was confronted again by the drawing of the face that had confronted him the day before the flight. And he put the book down on the steps. Enough, if anyone wants to read let him go ahead and read, he thought. I'm sick and tired of these books, enough. What a torment. Leave me alone, he thought.

Someone sat down next to him on the steps. He peeked at the drawing on the page. English? English? You want to see the cathedral? You want to see the secret fresco? You want to see the new catacombs?

Yoel went on staring at the drawing, as if he didn't realize that the man was talking to him. He looked round. A black man of about forty was sitting there, pointing at the drawing lying on the step next to Yoel. He said something in a language Yoel didn't understand. Swahili? Yoel guessed. Si, si, the man's eyes lit up. You want to see the new catacombs? All legal. And he took out a crumpled document in a plastic cover, with an official stamp on it.

Yoel handed him a hundred euro note. Let him take it and leave him alone. He always gave alms in foreign cities, he felt it was a true connection to the city, and he always dreamed of being able to give a huge sum, but for years Leah wouldn't let him, and after she died, well, by then he was already used to it. The man, who introduced himself as Frederick, said that he was very sorry, he didn't have any change. But down in the catacombs, behind the fresco that they weren't showing to tourists yet, there were two friends of his, and one of them would definitely have change. Lots of coins, lots of new coins, he said, and for some reason he raised his hand and pointed to the moon.

Yoel refused politely. In two hours time he had to leave for the airport. But two hours, sir, this is a once-in-a-lifetime opportunity, and the tour lasts twenty minutes, and he would get coffee down there, what a question! Let me explain, we're talking about a site that hasn't been opened to tourists yet, said Frederick, the place is still in preparation for the opening, in six months' time they'll open it and then the queue will be as long as for the Vatican, and it will cost a lot to go in, fifty euro, and of course taking photographs will be forbidden, and here you have a once-in-a-lifetime opportunity to see an unknown fresco by Piero in peace and quiet, effused the guide, and the Roman tombs that haven't seen the light for two thousand years, nobody's seen them . . . and there could be photographs . . . of course, he, Frederick, how to put it, was in charge of the place . . . on guard in the afternoon, after the restoration workers left . . . and the coffee downstairs was hot . . . fresh . . .

As in a dream Yoel found himself gliding obliquely over the wide piazza, Frederic holding his arm, his hand pleasant to the touch. Suddenly Yoel realized that the drawing of Leah's face was gone. He must have forgotten it on the steps with the book, he thought sorrowfully, but going back now would be pointless, the page had certainly been blown away by the wind or thrown away by the sanitation people. And he saw it crumpled in a bin, creased and dirty, buried under heaps of tourist trash, and likewise the book. He'll draw me another one, Yoel muttered to himself in a whisper, even though Emile was already thirty seven years old and could no longer draw like that.

Next to the magnificent entrance to the Duomo the guide turned left and started walking along the wall—his hand still on Yoel's arm. Yoel run the fingers of his free hand over the stones. And it seemed that there was no end to the wall. Yoel closed his eyes and allowed his guide to lead him. Suddenly he rejoiced in the word itself, "guide," and he said "guide, guide" almost aloud. He still had time until the night flight, he would be able to stay here as long as he wanted to. And his spirits rose. Instead of his last hours here being a waste, an attraction like this had come his way. And there was no need for unreasonable suspicions. Be trusting, be trusting. At last something you didn't find in tourist guides. At last a corner of this city that hadn't been mapped, that hadn't been given marks. And an unknown fresco by Piero della Francesca, he thought, of course he had heard of this painter, of course, one of the famous names. It was really fantastic, and already he thought of a few art-loving friends who would marvel at his pictures. The batteries in his camera were charged. And the coffee—local coffee, fresh coffee, and of course, the new catacombs.

After a few seconds the guide stopped. The rear of the cathedral was very different from the front. As if the vast church had been divided between two areas of jurisdiction, two cities. In front was the rich, clean, tourist city. In the back the cathedral bordered on a slum, there were sheets hanging from the balconies, huge piles of garbage, and horses harnessed to tourist carriages from the nineteenth century stood and dropped dung. Masons were working on a big block of stone. Grooms in patched and tattered liveries enjoyed their afternoon break there. Ravens pecked at broken pomegranates.

The guide said something about a sanitation workers strike, about pensioners looking for work as carriage drivers for tourists. Politely but firmly he tried to turn Yoel's attention from this neighborhood to the back wall of the cathedral. He drew him there with the tips of his fingers. After a few steps there appeared before him a small opening, very low, like a door, half of which was below street level and half above it. The guide signaled Yoel to go down on his hands and knees and crawl in backward.

The minute he entered the opening, with his back to the interior, a plastic protective helmet with a lamp set in its front was dropped onto his head. He descended the ladder left against the wall by the people working on the site. His lamp illuminated the rungs of the ladder and the damp wall behind it. Above his head he saw the bare pale soles of the guide. He asked him how much farther down they had to go. The guide didn't reply.

When they reached the bottom, Yoel began to regret the whole thing. It was clear that a little Roman area had been discovered here, even a whole town, over which the cathedral of Milan had been built. The guide reached the ground. They took a few steps inside and the guide tapped on Yoel's forehead and shouted something in Swahili, and then he said in English, I forgot, what an idiot, I forgot the key to the catacombs upstairs, with Giovanni. Yoel didn't have the strength to ask who Giovanni was, and he knew that he had no intention of climbing up and down the ladder again. There was something not quite right about all this. Although only few minutes had passed since this unique expedition had begun, he did not, on any account, want to risk being late for his flight. He turned the lamp on his head toward the guide and said, it doesn't matter, it's not important, we can do without the catacombs, and make do with the fresco. But the guide put up his hand and switched on the lamp on his own helmet and said, that's impossible, that's impossible, the fresco is in the heart of the burial complex. You wouldn't want to see the fresco through a dense grille, signor!

They stood there for a moment in silence. The guide took off his helmet and cleaned it. The light flickered over the walls. This was his suggestion: Yoel should take a few more steps, just two minutes of slow walking in all. At the end of the short path ahead he would find the brothers who would give him a short explanation of the site, which he needed to get in any case, and by the time they were done the guide would already be back with the key. Yoel fixed anxious eyes on the guide. And what if this Giovanni wasn't around? But the guide only laughed. Giovanni wasn't going anywhere, he was a cripple, a beggar who sat outside the cathedral and played the zither, wearing a fez, and kept the key round his neck. Forty strings, the guide stressed proudly, forty strings, and ran his fingers over his shining helmet as if he himself was plucking each and every one of them. And in any case, the guide took Yoel's hand in both his kindly hands, in any case, the children are here, I have to come back anyway to get them. And again his eyes lit up. That's your guarantee, he laughed, like Simon in the Bible, yes? And to Yoel's horror he took Emile's drawing out of his pocket and smoothed it out and showed it to Yoel, as if there was nothing more natural, as if Yoel had given it to him as a gift. And perhaps he really had given it to him, without thinking about what he was doing? And while Yoel was searching for words the guide shouted something into the passage and climbed quickly up the ladder.

Yoel turned back. The underground hall was illuminated, and already showed signs of preparation for the tourists who would soon be arriving. Silver air-conditioning pipes had already been installed, a few blank notices already hung on the walls, waiting for the explanations that would be stamped on them. A big red digital clock had already been set in a prominent place. A rail had already been fixed on the wall, and Yoel put his hand on it and started walking. Suddenly he felt joy and relief. Perhaps because the walking reminded him of the youth-movement hikes and the hikes with friends he'd taken sometime in the late forties, when they would run off, children of fifteen, sleeping in the fields, descending into this or that cave, dreaming of the train to Lebanon, dreaming of the train to Damascus, to Baghdad, making up stories of their travels deep into the British Mandate territories, joking with Australian and British soldiers, eagerly taking proffered shillings, cracking open watermelons where they grew, returning home after three or four days, his parents hadn't even noticed his absence, eating their midday meal, his father buried in the newspaper, his mother massaging her temples.

Yoel advanced along the passage. A number of plasma screens had already been installed, ready for presentations. From time to time he saw himself reflected in the dark screens, and he even stopped for a moment in order to examine his face in one of them. The light of his headlamp glinted in the screens. He fixed his hair. And when he turned his head the child was already there.

The child sat on a high cashier's stool, huddled in a very big coat like a blanket, holding an iron cashbox for selling tickets, leaning against the rather dense mesh of an iron grille, behind which it was indeed possible to make out a few tombs and a large mural shrouded in darkness. Only then did Yoel realize that the child was sleeping, his head resting against the grille. The other brother was nowhere to be seen. Yoel stood still. He was afraid to make a sound, reluctant to wake the child and startle him. On the other hand, the boy would be accustomed to occasional visitors, but still, but still. He was a child of about ten, dark but not like his father. His hair was quite fair and smooth, and it was clear that his mother was white. A cold drop of water fell from the ceiling and landed on Yoel's helmet. Under the child's stool lay a pair of little crutches.

Yoel stood still. Better to wait for the father to come back. Not to wake the child. In any case, the gate was still closed. He would do without the lecture. What could the child explain anyway. And did he even know English at all. The whole thing was nonsense.

Then there was a sound behind him. He relaxed, the father's already back, he thought, barely five minutes have passed. The clatter of clogs advanced down the passageway, and Yoel wanted to hush the father, so as not to wake the child. But to his surprise it wasn't the father, Frederick, but a fair woman, apparently a German, and Yoel understood immediately that she was the child's mother. The woman apologized, Frederick had been detained upstairs, he didn't want to keep Yoel waiting, she had brought him the key.

The woman saw that the child was sleeping. She went up to him and put her hand on his head. The child opened his eyes and for a moment he looked at Yoel as if his dream was continuing before his eyes, and then he blinked. Yoel raised his hand to cover his headlamp and smiled. The child opened the iron box and handed him a ticket. Yoel saw that the ticket didn't belong to this site, that it was a very old ticket, and the price on it was in liras, it must be an old ticket from some other tourist attraction. But he didn't care. He handed the child a hundred euro note. The child gave him back a fifty and closed the box.

In the painting a woman was standing inside a kind of tent whose lining emulated a stone wall, and on either side of her were symmetrical angels opening or perhaps closing the flaps of the tent. Her eyelids were slightly lowered, her hand pointed to a slit in her dress, her other hand rested curled on her waist. Yoel went inside and first he took a few steps between the tombs, trying not to look at his watch. The tombs were decorated with paintings of flowers and animals, and after regarding them dutifully, in order "not to insult" them, Yoel approached the wall. His nose almost touched the big painting. The colors were vivid, they looked so fresh it seemed they would smudge if he touched them. He glanced behind him. The mother and child looked rather bored and took no notice of him. His headlamp drilled into the painted woman's mouth with a narrow beam. And Yoel slowly lifted his hand, taking care to hide it with his body. He brought his finger closer to the body of the painted woman, whose half-closed eyes, slightly higher than he was, seemed to be looking straight at him. He sent his finger to the white slit in her dress. He touched the white, and ran his finger up it. Rough white, he murmured. Rough white. He was very close, his whole body. He wanted to spread out his arms and cover the faces of the angels with his hands. To press his lips against the slit in the dress. He didn't want to see, he couldn't see, he was so close. But someone sounded an alarm, perhaps some electronic eye had activated it automatically, if belatedly, and Yoel recoiled, to confront the reproachful looks of the German woman and her son. The German woman came up and pulled him away to stop the nagging whine of the alarm.

And sticking out of the child's pocket, Yoel saw the page torn from the notebook with Emile's drawing, folded into four, regarding him with one eye. The boy's father presumably stole toys and souvenirs from the tourists to give to his son. Yoel wanted to scold him, but he put his hand on his head instead. He had already forgotten the hot coffee. All he wanted was to get out of there. And indeed, the mother hoisted the child on her back. Without being asked, Yoel picked up the little crutches and tucked them under his arm. They were so light. And so the two of them, that is to say the three of them, advanced to the other end of the passage and started to climb the ladder. He held on with one hand and climbed. The light of the lamp on his helmet went out. His white fingertip shone faintly in the dark, skipping from rung to rung above him. And then, below his feet, he heard the second child coming up behind him.

III

YOEL–EMILE

And he went home and decided that as soon as he walked in the door he would phone Emile and tell him at last how he had thought of giving him back and how earlier that day he had visited the parents in their apartment. And when he reached the street he saw Emile, walking toward the house and singing to himself. And he walked quietly for a while behind his walking boy, as he had walked behind him thirty years before, on exactly the same paving stones. Until he called him. And Emile turned round and smiled, and said, "I was just thinking about you," and took out his white earphones. And Yoel asked him if he wanted to go for a drive, and they got into the car and drove without talking. Until Emile, who shortly before then had seen the singer Shlomo Artzi walking down the avenue holding an electric guitar, said to Yoel, "You won't believe who I saw on our street." But Yoel didn't ask who.

For a moment Yoel thought of going back to the parents' apartment, just driving past it in the road. Had they pulled down the building already. You could do it so quickly. In an hour. Bull-dozer, dynamite. He had the feeling that if they only drove past, Emile and him together, something would happen. The father or the mother would still be there. And they would recognize him. Them. And even if they didn't. He felt as if the meeting had to take place. A touch. A look. Just not this same distance. And he saw how he was already driving slowly by on the bridge, and slowing down as he passed all the dirty shutters, and the window open-ing as he touched the brakes. And then he sped up. And Emile gave him a long look and then he said, "Daddy," and Yoel, who was completely wrapped up in himself, let out a kind of "Ha," and Emile looked at him and said, "Tell me, why were you walking round like that," and Yoel said, "What? what do you mean?" And Emile examined him for a moment and then he said, "Like, with this blanket around your shoulders?" and took the edge of the checked blanket between two fingers, and Yoel was stunned but inhaled and replied, "Oh, that," and his lips tightened for a mo-ment, and then he said, "It's for you," and abruptly made a U-turn on an orange light and began to head back.

LEAH

I knew who it would be even before I went in. I couldn't describe him but I recognized him immediately. When the door opened and they went in she didn't look away, didn't turn off to the side. Her eyes opened into the eyes of the child and he looked back at her as if his name had been called at the far end of the room. And Yoel followed her look and said, "That one?" with obvious reservations, they'd agreed on a girl, and then why such a dark one . . .

And somebody said (Yoel remembered) that he had been born two days ago, he was brand new, didn't know anything yet, didn't have a clue. And Leah looked at him, and he lowered his eyes, and she went up to the cot, and read the name of her son in a whisper. And again she tried to work out when she would, ostensibly, have been pregnant. Just in case she was asked. So she would have her answer ready. And even before they left the parking lot of the adoption agency attached to the maternity hospital, they gave him, for the time being, the name that the two parents who had abandoned him had given him. They had left a note stuck to his diaper, or so the nurse had told them. Only one word. But the note had been lost. Lucky they'd copied the name down in time.

And he looked at the sleeping child and said quietly, as if nursing a faint doubt: Emile? And then, again, as if stating a fact, as if by the power of speech the child had been created, there in that taxi. And the driver asked her, sitting next to her, in a Russian accent, "Was it a difficult birth?" And she said to him, "Certainly not, I hardly felt a thing," and Yoel, in the back seat, said, "Yes, neither did I."

YOEL–EMILE

Emile played at being a waiter. He came with a tray and a glass of water. And Yoel drank the cold water. And he asked for another glass. And Emile brought it. And he knew that he would bring him more and more glasses, as many as he wanted, and that he too, Yoel, would have brought him, Emile, as many glasses of water as he wanted, in the same glass, on that tray. And he said so to Emile, but Emile was busy concentrating on his game and asked if his father wanted the check, and Yoel thought for a minute and said, "Yes. Daddy wants it. Thank you, mister headwaiter," and Emile tore off the page and handed him the bill with a bow. And then Emile went to the kitchen and poured another one and went to the bedroom and put it down on the little bedside table, careful not to wake her. And indeed she didn't wake up.

THE CITY

A windswept desert planet, sand slithering like snakes over plains where something had once existed. The great red sun already takes up half the sky. Fills every gaze. But there are no gazes. If there were anyone to gaze at it they would have gone blind. Dust. Therefore no one sees. It's not good to see such things. It's not necessary to see everything. For a long time there's been nothing here. And a very long time will pass before there's anything new. A bird between two trees, one planted at each end of the world. But there will be, he suddenly thought, there will be, there will be, it's only a matter of time. Lucky we won't be here to wait for it to pass. We've been spared the wait. When it reaches that tree it will chirp and we'll wake up. One day we'll simply be here again. And I'll be his father again. Actually it's not so terrible, this whole arrangement, he thought, and closed the book, and set it down on the checked blanket folded on his lap, and put his hands on the cover of the book. The dog ran here and there, skipping around the father and son, spraying a little water back into the sea and onto his dark glasses. They threw him an old tennis ball and he ran to fetch it. The water rose a little and the son, without any effort at all, pulled his old father's wheelchair back a little, its wheels left two lines in the wet strip of sand, and after a moment they were wiped out.

EMILE

I'm standing opposite him and there's a door between us. Not locked, it can be opened on either side. On my side the light is very faint. I can see his side too, how strange. I can see it even though I'm here, on this side. The light on his side is brighter. Perhaps it's a mirage. Mine is a dim, yellow lamp light. His is the light of the midday sun. If I touch the handle of the door he will too. If I push the door with the tips of my fingers he'll make room and I'll go in. Is it a sliding door? I stand opposite the door. My name is written on the door, his name is probably written on it too, on the other side. And perhaps my name is written both here and there. But what is my name? He closes/I close the door on his side, on my side. The door stands in front of me, and I read my full name on the closed door. There is no door. His eye is dancing, wet, in the peephole. And perhaps it is my second eye.

Bill / glass of water: 0 NIS, glass of water: 0 NIS

HEBREW LITERATURE SERIES

The Hebrew Literature Series at Dalkey Archive Press makes available major works of Hebrew-language literature in English translation. Featuring exceptional authors at the forefront of Hebrew letters, the series aims to introduce the rich intellectual and aesthetic diversity of contemporary Hebrew writing and culture to English-language readers.

This series is published in collaboration with the Institute for the Translation of Hebrew Literature, at www.ithl.org.il. Thanks are also due to the Office of Cultural Affairs at the Consulate General of Israel, NY, for their support.

DROR BURSTEIN was born in 1970 in Netanya, Israel, and lives in Tel Aviv, where he teaches at Tel Aviv University. He has previously edited programs for Israel Radio's classical music station, and written literary and art reviews. He has been awarded the Bernstein Prize (2005) and the Prime Minister's Prize (2006).

DALYA BILU lives in Jerusalem and has been awarded a number of prizes for her translation work, including the Israeli Ministry of Culture Prize for Translation, and the Jewish Book Council Award for Hebrew-English Translation.